The REINCARNATION
Of HUT¢HER$

Can you will all of your assets to yourself for your
next life?

—————————————

by
Emmanuel Campbell

Cover design by Jessie Tickles

ISBN: 978-1-7372623-0-5

Dedication

This book is dedicated to my mother, who always taught her children we could do anything possible in this world. She taught us the value of life and morality, and we followed those rules to the best of our ability. Her humbleness and dedication to assisting others is something that I honor. Her selflessness has rubbed off on me in many ways. So this is for you, Mom, in all you do and have done for us and others. To my editor, James Gallagher, who helped give my story more depth. Jessie Tickles, you are amazing! You saw my vision and added your touch, which made the cover come to life. Last but not least, to my colleagues, family, and friends, who listened to my story lines and read chapters of the manuscript while encouraging me to continue.

Preface

This fictional tale came from a long-ago conversation with a colleague while we were taping a program. For one segment, the hosts interviewed a woman who practiced past-life regression and hypnosis for her clients. The next segment was an interview with an estate-planning lawyer. During my conversation with my colleague, I posed the question: What if you could will all your assets to yourself for your next life? After we stopped laughing at the idea, I came up with this tale. Although the following is fiction, it does pose a fascinating theory. I'm thankful that you decided to take this journey with me and explore this interesting "what if."

CHAPTERS

DREAMING

The iron gates outside a mansion in Bartlesville, Oklahoma, creaked and swayed in the wind as rain lashed the mansion's exterior. Inside the home, just before 11:00 p.m. on July 12, 1958, an old man sat at his desk, writing in his journal, the room lit only by the flickering of candles and intermittent flashes of lightning.

The man, Ferron Hutchers, placed his quill into the ink bottle and picked up the candelabra sitting next to him. He then began his nightly ritual, moving toward the stairway leading to his bedroom. As he climbed the steps, the old man clutched his heart and felt a sharp, stabbing pain explode in his chest. He lost his balance and dropped the candelabra onto the carpeted stairs, a small fire igniting around him.

The butler, on his way to bed, saw his boss struggling with the fire. He grabbed a couch covering to put out the flames but was too late to save the man. The stench of burned skin sickened the butler as he turned the old man over, gasping at the damage the fire had done to his boss's face.

At the same time of night, in an apartment in Edison, New Jersey, six decades later, a man sat straight up in bed and screamed. Walker Preston sweated profusely as he glanced around his dimly lit room. He looked at his alarm clock and noticed that it was four thirty in the morning. He'd only had a nightmare, except he'd had the same one before. In fact, he'd had it so many times he'd stopped counting. Walker grudgingly got out of bed, walked to his bathroom, closed the door, and turned on the shower.

***

Walker stood in a crowded elevator on his way to work at his accounting office of Michaels and McNair in Elizabeth, New Jersey. His five-foot-eleven frame looked rather handsome in the new navy-blue suit he'd just bought, but he was not thinking about how he looked today. In fact, he wore a hat over his dark-brown hair to try to hide the sleepless look on his face. He began thinking about the dream he'd had.

Preston saw a woman he knew and nodded to her with a slight smile. Sheila Crowder, one of Walker's closest friends—as well as his ex—knew about his nightmares and wouldn't fail to notice how tired he looked. She made her way past other passengers to the back of the elevator, where he was standing, and whispered to him.

"Boy, you really look like hell. What happened to you?"

Walker regarded her with his bloodshot eyes and mumbled something about having a bad night.

"Another nightmare, huh?"

Walker looked away. "Yeah, only this time, it seemed more real than the others."

"What are you going to do?" she asked.

The elevator stopped, and both got off with some of the other passengers.

"I don't know, but I have to do something."
They both stopped a few feet from the elevator and began speaking to each other more privately.

"You know, you really should see someone to help you analyze those dreams."

Walker turned and looked at her like he was a lost child. "I told you before, I'm not going to any shrink for some stupid little dreams. And besides, it's only one dream."

"Yeah, but it keeps happening again and again. Aren't you tired of it?"

"Well, it's been going on for most of my life, so I'm used to it now."

Sheila dug in her purse. "Well, it seems like it's getting worse. I have someone I think you should see." She found a business card and handed it to him.

Walker examined the card carefully. "What's this?"

"He's a psychologist named Dr. Steingold, and he's very good. I think he can help you."

Walker took the card and put it in his left breast pocket. "I keep telling you I don't need any help."

Sheila smiled at him as she walked away. "You do. You just hate to admit it."

Walker watched her walk away, and a smile crossed his face.

Walker made a stop at the men's room to make a final check of himself before going to his office. He went to the urinal to relieve himself, then walked toward the mirror. As he checked his hair, the reflection in the mirror changed into something familiar. It was the same study as in the mansion in his dream. Walker reached out to touch the mirror, but his hand went right through it as though the mirror were a pool of water. Walker stared at the image in front of him. He saw the same old man he had seen so many times in his dream, walking around in the study. Walker watched the scene as if he were watching a movie. He saw the old man walk sideways and closer to the edge of the mirror's image.

Just as quickly as the old man had appeared, he turned to the mirror and faced Walker with a horrid face. It was charred and smoldering, as if it had been placed on a bed of hot coals. The image terrified Walker so much that he broke out in a cold sweat, backed away, fell, and blacked out.

When Walker opened his eyes, the room appeared to be spinning with people and noise. He sat slumped in a chair, and he thought he heard someone yell about getting a doctor or some water. He started to come to his senses and noticed everyone standing around, examining him as though he'd had a terrible accident. The room began to focus, and the maze of empty cubicles around him came clear. A hard, husky voice was shouting commands.

"Give him some room; give him some air. Did someone get me that . . . wait, he's coming to."

Walker put his hand on his head. "Wha . . . what happened?"

The man who was shouting the orders studied him. "We don't know. I came into the men's room, and you were lying on the floor. You must've blacked out or something."

Walker tried to get up but felt light-headed and stumbled forward. The man caught him as he began to fall.

"Whoa, slow down. Take it easy and sit for a while."

Walker saw Sheila hurrying from the back of the crowd to get to him. She hugged him. "Are you okay?"

Walker hugged her back. "I think so. We need to talk."

"When?"

"ASAP!"

"I'll be at my desk when you're ready. How about lunch?"

"Okay, but we need to go somewhere and walk. I don't think I can eat right now."

"Fine, but it's a good thing I brought a sandwich today."

Walker got up and went to his office with everybody watching him. He turned around to face them. "I'm all right. Thanks for being concerned, but we all have work to do, don't we?"

Walker's manager came over to him and patted him on the shoulder. "Look, if you need to take the day off, do so."

"No, that's okay. I have this big project coming up, and I really need to work on it."

"Whatever you say, but if at any time . . ."

"Look, I'm fine. I can get through the day."

Walker was getting a little perturbed at the whole situation and wished it had never happened. His manager shrugged, turned around, and walked to his office.

Time flew by as Walker worked. He was unaware of everything happening around him until he heard a light knock on the doorjamb and smelled something faint but pleasant. As he looked up, a smile appeared across his face. The sight was as great as the scent. This was the first time he'd really taken notice of Sheila since they'd stopped dating. The green dress she wore on her curvy five-foot-seven frame complemented her green eyes, which he remembered gazing into for such long periods of time. He imagined his hands going through her hair as he kissed her lips. Walker could not believe that he'd let her get out of his life because he was not ready for a serious relationship. But he was glad they were still good friends.

"Are you ready?" she said as she stood in front of him.

"Yeah, let me put this away, and we can get going. What time is it, anyway?"

"It's twelve thirty. I thought I would give you some extra time to get some work done."

He smiled and remembered how considerate she had always been. *Boy, I must have really been stupid to leave her,* he thought to himself, *but I can't dwell on it.* Walker signed off, closed his laptop, and slowly got up. He came from behind his desk and headed toward the door with Sheila.

It was warm outside, and a slight breeze brushed across their faces as they strolled down the busy street. Walker and Sheila laughed and joked about things that would not make much sense to anyone else—mostly because he was trying to avoid the subject at hand.

They found their way to the park two blocks from their office building. They looked for somewhere to sit. Everyone seemed to be out enjoying the weather. No matter where they searched, they could not find an empty bench. Finally, Walker and Sheila laid eyes on a nice, isolated area with a tree hovering over a bench. Walker waited until Sheila sat; then he sat next to her. He became quiet and put his head down, then gave a deep sigh. Sheila saw this as a sign that he was ready to talk.

"Soooo . . . what is it that you wanted to talk to me about?" she probed.

Walker raised his head with a sullen look.

"Well, like I told you earlier, my dreams have been

getting worse. Sometimes it feels as though I'm living in those dreams, and it seems more like reality than anything else."

"What do you mean?"

Walker hesitated to tell her this part, but he thought that if anyone would believe and not ridicule him, it would be Sheila. So he took a deep breath and began. "Remember this morning when I was found in the men's room?"

"Uh-huh."

"Well, I saw something that really scared the hell out of me. I was standing in front of the mirror, and it turned into one of the scenes from my dream. I know it sounds weird, but I can't explain it myself. You may think I'm crazy, but this is really getting out of hand. I don't know what's going to happen next, and for that matter, I'm scared to think of it."

As he was talking, Walker's surroundings faded into a blur as he told Sheila the story of what he'd seen and how the old man had appeared to him in the mirror.

Walker kept explaining his situation. "The funny thing is that it seems like every time I see this guy, I get the strange feeling that I know him. Maybe it's because I have seen him so many times. I just don't know what's happening."

Walker looked at Sheila and wondered if she thought he was just hallucinating. He figured, of all people, she would believe him because they'd known each other for two years, but then this whole ordeal seemed too strange, even for him.

Sheila brought up the subject about the psychologist again. "Have you honestly thought about seeing Dr. Steingold?"

"Who?"

"Dr. Steingold. You know, the one on the card I gave you this morning."

"Oh yeah, uh, I just don't know. Shrinks always scared the daylights out of me. I don't think I could go through with it. They're always trying to probe your mind. I'll probably tell him my problems, and the next thing you know, I'll be labeled as a fruitcake."

"Well, it wouldn't hurt to go, and it's not as bad as you might think. They try to make you feel very relaxed and comfortable before they start with the session."

"You sound like you've been before."

"No, but if you would like me to come with you, I wouldn't mind."

"Gee, thanks," Walker said with a laugh, "just what I need: someone to listen and another to question me."

"Oh, come on," Sheila said while elbowing him, "what are friends for?"

He looked at her and took her by the hand. "And you're a good friend too. Thanks for being there."

He helped her up, and they began to stroll back to the office.

REMEMBRANCE

Ferron M. Hutchers came into the world in 1882 as a middle-class boy in New London, Connecticut. He lived in the small town in a two-room house shared by his mother, Nancy; his father, Errol; and his older brother, Robert. Ferron's life was simple and happy—that is, until his father went to work one day and disappeared without a trace. Ferron was five at the time. His mother became so depressed that she stopped her life. No cleaning, washing, or tending to her children, to herself, or to the home. She cooked only when necessary, and to her, that was a pain. She felt that since Robert was nine, he was old enough to take care of himself and his little brother.

Four years after their father left, Robert decided to take Ferron to the lake and do some fishing. He went to ask his mother if it was okay but saw her in the kitchen, sitting in that same dazed state she could never seem to shake. So he decided not to ask. He took his little brother, Ferron, and went to the lake with rod and fishing gear in hand.

Robert had planned on fishing at the edge of the pier until he saw a small, empty boat inviting him and his brother to take it out in the water. He helped Ferron into the small craft and pushed it off the shore. Robert paddled until he felt he was far enough to make a good catch. Ferron was excited about being far off into the water, but the excitement wore off, and as time drifted, so did he. Ferron was resting peacefully until he felt himself roll and hit the side of the boat. Robert was fighting with his rod and reel, pulling back, pushing forward. He had something caught on the other end of his line.

"Ferron, help me reel this sucker in! Wow! Hurry! I can't hold on much longer!"

Ferron was still too groggy to understand what was happening, but he began to crawl over to his big brother. Just as he was about to reach him, Robert lost his balance and fell forward. Ferron's hand touched the back of Robert's left sneaker just before his brother went face-first into the water. "Noooooooooooo! Roooooooberrrrrt! Noooooooooooo!"

Ferron looked on both sides of the boat but could see no sign of his only brother—and his only friend. He moved to the front of the boat and saw the fishing reel off in the distance, turning slowly in a circle. Then it sank into the lake. As Ferron glanced about, Robert surfaced, panicking, and thrashing about. But his futile attempts only pushed him farther from the boat, and he sank again below the surface. Ferron sat back in the boat, too shocked and scared to move. He stayed that way until the boat's owner came to retrieve him.

Ferron arrived at home with a police escort and a blanket wrapped around him. His mother was still sitting where they'd left her. She appeared to stare into space as the officer told her about the accident. She seemed not to register any response to the tragic details the officer gave her. Ferron saw the cop talking to his mother but realized the cop had not noticed her state when they'd arrived at the house.

"Ma'am, are you okay?" The cop gently shook his mother. "Did you hear me? Your son Rober—"

The cop's voice trailed off as he took her hand. "Bill, get the kid outa here. His mother's not in too great of shape either."

The other cop, who was standing alongside Ferron, looked lazily at his partner.

"Bill!" the first cop yelled, pointing at the kid, and thumbing an authoritative gesture to the door.

Bill looked at the lady in the chair and finally seemed to realize what his partner was so anxious about. He hurried Ferron out the kitchen door and sat him on the steps. But Ferron had also seen what was wrong. Even though he did not understand it, he somehow knew he was a nine-year-old without a soul to care for him.

Although Ferron's mother had three brothers and two sisters, no one wanted to take him in because they "had enough kids and too many damn problems of their own," so Ferron was placed in an orphanage. Once there, no one at the orphanage talked to him— partly because he was new, but more so because he was quiet and kept to himself.

When it was time to play, he would huddle up in a corner and stare into space as though he were searching for something. He was looking for someone to come talk to him, someone to come give him a hug. But no one did so. Not even the staff. This made him aware that he was very alone and very lonely. This also made him aware that, at such a young age, he would have to take care of himself, because no one else wanted to. Ferron began closing out all that made everyone else happy, because their joys were his pain, their laughter his sadness, and their ecstasy his envy.

Four years passed as Ferron stayed in the orphanage. He was still as lonely as the first day he was placed there. They said he would like it and adjust well with the other children. They said that maybe, just maybe, someone would come out and want him to live with them. They said . . . they said . . . but none of it came true. No friends, no prospects who came by to see if they would like to keep him for a weekend or even for a day. Nothing "they" said made any difference anyway. He had already set in his mind that he had to look out for himself—starting now. He was only thirteen, but that did not matter to him. He knew it was time to go. Since he figured no one wanted him, including his family, he surmised he wouldn't be missed.

I'll wait till night, when everyone's asleep, and get out of here. Who'll know? Who'll miss me? These thoughts played in his head until nightfall.

Ferron took his bedsheets and stuffed them inside his pillowcase. He slid out of bed slowly so the usual creaks would not disturb anyone's sleep and botch his getaway. He saw the hallway light was still on. The night shift was making their rounds, and they'd left his room a few minutes before. He knew that once they finished rounds, he could take his time and get out, but he hungered to leave this godforsaken place as soon as possible.

Earlier, when everyone else was eating supper, he'd excused himself with a "pain in his stomach" and had said he wanted to go to his room. Ferron had taken a sack of food he had been storing for this occasion and had placed it out a window behind some bushes, so no one would see it. Now, the only thing that stopped him were the people in the hall, and they wouldn't be there for long. A few minutes later, the hall lights went dim. To the night shift, it was normal procedure, but to Ferron, it was his signal that it was time to leave.

The door slowly opened, and he saw his pathway to freedom. He closed the door and walked close to the wall so he wouldn't cast a shadow. When he saw that no one was in the hall, he ran as fast as he could to the window, opened it, and slid out. The air was cool for July, but that did not matter. Ferron Hutchers was glad to be out in the night. He went to the bushes to retrieve his sack of hidden food and headed toward the open field. He was young and free!

NEW BEGINNING/ENDING LESSON

Ferron found himself in a moving boxcar on his way to anywhere. He knew he could not be the little boy huddled in a corner anymore. He now had to be much older than he wanted, and even though he was alone, Ferron was happy. Happy to be alone with no one to bother him. As the boxcar rode the noisy track, the clickety-clack of the train lulled Ferron to sleep.

He was awakened with a strange feeling. A feeling that someone was watching him. No, not watching, but staring. He looked around and saw a man sitting in the far opposite side of the boxcar. Ferron jumped up, grabbed his sack of food, and hugged it as if it were a teddy bear.

"Relax, relax, lil' buddy. I'm not gonna hurt cha. What ya got there?" The old man stood up and wobbled with the movement of the boxcar and started toward Ferron. His gray beard looked as though it had not been shaved in a few days, and his clothes were torn and patched, with one suspender hanging down. Ferron was wide eyed as the old man stepped closer. But he was not afraid. He was startled because he'd thought he was the only person there.

As the man came closer, Ferron could smell the week-old stench the man carried.

"Whus ya name, boy?"

"F-F-Ferron."

"F-F-Ferron, huh? That's a weird one. Why all the *F*s in front of your name?" The old man smiled as he talked, and Ferron started to relax.

"Ferron, my name is Ferron," he stated more firmly.

"Oh, that's better, but it's still weird. The name's McRoss, Pete McRoss, but you can call me Rossy. That's what my friends call me."

He extended his hand for Ferron to shake. Ferron looked at him with suspicion. "What makes you think

I'm your friend? I don't *know* you."

Rossy looked at him and the bag. "Because if you're riding in here all alone, you're gonna need one. Where ya from?"

"Does it matter?"

"No, just trying to make conversation." He slyly looked again at the bag, but Ferron did not notice.

"Had anything to eat lately?"

Ferron looked at Rossy, then the bag. Rossy watched his every move, like a con man ready for his victim.

"Uh, yeah, I did. Before I got on." Ferron was trying to hide the fact that he had food, but it didn't work.

"Well, I think you should have some food now, since you have a bagful."

"How did you know?" Ferron immediately started to distrust Rossy.

"Well," said Rossy, "you told me."

"I never said a word."

"You didn't have to." Rossy pointed to the bag. "I asked you a question and watched your response. Oldest trick in the book. You held on tighter to the bag when I asked you about food. I could've stolen the whole bag from you when you went back to sleep, but I won't. You look lost, and I want to help you survive. We can help each other, and you can start by letting me have some food."

Ferron loosened the bag from his chest and gave it to Rossy. He knew he was telling the truth and was glad of it.

Rossy took the bag, pulled out some food, and gave the bag back to Ferron. "First lesson: don't give nobody somethin' for nothin'. The food is payment for what I just told you. Just follow my lead and you'll do fine. Just fine indeed."

And so began Ferron's lessons in life.

Three years passed, and Ferron had learned many things from Rossy, who eagerly taught the lessons to him, but for one, which he was saving. Ferron learned not only how to read a person by their gestures and actions but how to take no mercy when he bought, sold, traded . . . or whatever they did to help them survive. He had no emotions toward anyone, except for ole Pete McRoss, who taught him everything at such a young age. With the schemes they played and the evenhanded business between each other, he had more than enough money to do what he wanted. Pete McRoss also taught him two other important lessons he wouldn't forget till the day he died, and even after that: never spend what you don't need to, and never, never give money away. Do so only as a loan and then at a high rate of interest, to make it worth your while.

Rossy and Ferron were staying at a boardinghouse they frequented when they were in this part of Texas. The two were having a late supper at a table set up outside the boardinghouse as they talked about their past deeds and adventures.

After supper, Rossy took out two identical boxes. One belonged to him and the other to Ferron. "Well, Ferron, I think you've become quite a young businessman, but I'm too old to continue." He watched Ferron's reaction closely, but Ferron maintained a stone-faced expression. Rossy had taught him this, and even though the pit of his stomach felt like boiling water and his heart was sinking, Ferron knew not to let Rossy know how he felt.

"You're good, Ferron, real good." He took the two boxes and opened them. "What I have here is an equal share of what we've made since we've been together, minus our expenses, of course. As you will see, it has been very profitable."

Ferron took both boxes and counted everything, then put it all back. Just as he was supposed to do. Rossy handed Ferron one of the boxes.

"This is for you."

Ferron took the box and set it at his side. "I'm sorry you have to leave me, but I do understand."

Ferron stuck out his hand to shake Rossy's, just as Rossy had taught him, and talked with such businesslike manners that it was eerie. If anyone had been watching, they would not have known these two were friends and partners who had depended on each other for the last three years. They would have thought it was just another business transaction that had just been settled. Rossy stood up and knocked down his box, and some of the contents spilled out. Ferron bent down to pick up the box and the spilled items for his friend. While Ferron was doing this, Rossy switched Ferron's box with a third one, which he had been hiding.

As Ferron handed Rossy his box, Rossy finished

the rest of his farewell speech: "Well, my good young man, I bid you farewell and good luck for the rest of your life." Rossy turned and walked away into the darkness, never to be seen again.

An hour passed before Ferron decided to look into his box again. When he did, he was astonished at the contents. It contained a small amount of money, strips of old newspaper, rocks, and a note.

Dear Ferron,

By now, you obviously have opened your box and found what's inside. I want you to know that I enjoyed having you as a pupil and loved watching you learn and grow. There is, however, one last trick and lesson I needed to teach you. Last trick . . . bait and switch. Last lesson . . . never let anyone or anything out of your sight until they have left from your view. Just to show you that I'm a nice guy, here's a deed to some land I traded for long ago. It's a worthless piece, but I'm sure you'll find a way to get rid of it. Good luck with the rest of your life.

Pete McRoss

Ferron was in shock, becoming dismayed, then angry. How could his only friend in the world do this to him? His heart became cold as he cried, because he knew he had been duped. Now with little money and a deed to a property he knew nothing about, he felt alone again. The only thing left for Ferron was to find this property and see if he could turn some kind of profit from it and get along with his life. He studied the deed and saw that the land was in Bartlesville, Oklahoma. It was getting late, so he decided to stay put for the night and begin his journey in the morning. As he lay down, he could not stop thinking about how his only friend almost made him penniless.

After all the jobs we did together, I can't believe he would do this to me, he thought as he lay sleepless, staring at the ceiling.

How am I supposed to trust anyone now? I thought he was a friend I could depend on for life, but I guess he showed me. From this day forward, I will no longer let anyone get that close to me again! These thoughts circled in his mind as he finally started to drift off to sleep.

The next morning, Ferron was up and ready to begin his life alone . . . again. But this time he had purpose. He gathered his belongings and went to pay the boarding fee, but he found Rossy had already taken care of it. *That's the least he could've done, since he took all my earnings,* he thought. Ferron saddled up and strapped the little possessions he had left to his name onto his horse and straddled it to begin his journey to Oklahoma.

Along the way, he never missed an opportunity to barter, trade, or swindle. What did he care? *These suckers were asking for it,* he thought. Now that he was on his own, he found that it was much easier to pull at people's heartstrings, because everyone thought of him as a young, innocent lad. Little did they know that he had experience beyond his years. He once pleaded with a traveling salesperson—or a bagman, as you will, who was selling nothing but worthless snake oil for pain remedies—to give him a couple of small gold nuggets for a pouch of pyrite. He told Mr. Snake Oil Man that the pouch had belonged to his father, who had been killed by bandits. His father had given him the pouch of "gold" because he knew the thieves wouldn't imagine him carrying something so valuable.

And now he was scared because it would be too dangerous for a boy his age to carry such a large amount of "gold," and he needed only enough to survive.

"So, mister, if you can give me two or three small nuggets that I can hide and carry, it would do a great deal for my safety."

The bagman, always looking for a deal, figured this was the opportunity of a lifetime, one he could not pass up. How lucky for him to get a naive young boy to offer him so much for so little. So he gladly accepted the offer and made the trade. As Ferron rode off with the three nuggets, both he and the traveling salesperson had the same thought: *What a sap!* But Ferron knew and thought to himself, *Once Mr. Snake Oil Man goes to reap his profit off the pouch, he's gonna be one sore loser.* He laughed as he realized he had skills that could carry him over for the rest of his life, and no one would *ever* be able to swindle him again. Not Ferron Hutchers . . . not ever.

Ferron finally arrived in Bartlesville, Oklahoma. He found the land that was swindled to him. There was a shack on the property so dilapidated that it looked as though it shouldn't still be standing. As he peered around the barren place, he noticed that nothing seemed to grow there but for a few patches of weeds scattered about. His heart sank even more when he saw how dismal this could be.

Well, he thought, *I may as well go in and see what I can do to get rid of this place.*

Ferron dismounted his horse and strode to the shack. As he stood in front of it, he noticed holes in the roof. Luckily, it was not the season for rain. Otherwise Ferron would have felt even more miserable.

He gathered his belongings and went inside. The place was actually better looking on the inside than he would've thought. There was a cot sitting against the wall. A woodburning stove sat in the middle of the room. The smokestack for the stove was partially intact, but it was something that could easily be fixed if he really needed to use it. Firewood was stacked against another wall, with cooking utensils lined up on a counter. *At least I can start a fire and keep warm, if need be,* he thought.

There were other things there he was glad to see:

tools, a few unopened cans of food . . . beans, tomatoes, mixed fruit, and vegetables. He also noticed a barrel in the corner with some clean, potable water. He took inventory and figured that with this and what he had with him, he would be able to sustain himself for a while.

Ferron got to work with cleaning the place to make it feel livable, for the moment. After all, he was not planning on staying long. Just enough time to get rid of this dump and move on. He was so focused on his thoughts that by the time he'd finished, he'd done more than he realized. But now he was tired, and it was getting late. Ferron almost forgot about his horse, so he fetched water out of the barrel to give to him and fed the horse some of the oats, apples, and peaches that he liked so much. Ferron sat down and opened his bag of provisions, which he'd brought with him, and ate a meal of beef jerky, rice, and potatoes. Afterward, he got his blanket, laid on the cot, and fell fast asleep.

Ferron woke up the next morning on a mission. His plan was to go into town and find someone to appraise this worthless place and get rid of it as soon as possible so he could move on with his life. He prepared his horse and rode into town. As he looked around, he finally saw what he was looking for. It was a sign:

Wilt Bourg—Arpenteur
I appraise your property for the best value

Ferron got off his horse, tied him to the nearest hitching post, and walked into the shop. He saw the man he assumed was Wilt sitting at a desk, looking over surveying maps. Ferron walked in slowly, noticing the surroundings and trying to get a feel of the place and the man.

"Uh, excuse me. Sir?" Ferron said with a slight voice, slighter than he noticed or realized.

"Yeah, what is it?" asked Wilt without even looking up from his work.

"I . . . have some land that I need appraised."

Wilt looked up with his glasses hanging from his nose and stared at Ferron. "You, boy? You have land, you say?" he asked with a slight chuckle. "And where is this . . . land that you say you have . . .

bothering me with such nonsense?"

Ferron was feeling a little agitated, not letting his

confidence take over as he was taught, but he was in strange territory and wasn't sure of himself. Although he was nervous, he began his rehearsed lines.

"My . . . my pa died while we were traveling. Before he did, he gave me this piece of paper and told me that it was for some land or something. I don't know. I really have no use for it, and since I'm alone, there's no need for me to stay here. I was wondering if you could appraise it and possibly sell it for me."

Wilt looked at Ferron with an eye of concern, but also with the possibility of making some easy money.

"Let me see what you got. What's your name, lad?"

"Ferron."

Ferron handed the deed to Wilt the arpenteur and watched him as he studied the document.

"Says here that you have ten acres of land. And you want to sell it?"

"Yes . . . sir. I wouldn't know what to do with it if I kept it."

"How old are you, son?" Wilt asked, trying to look caring.

"Sixteen, Mr. Bourg."

"Call me Wilt, easier to pronounce. I may be able to help you. Where's the land?"

"It's about ten miles or so that way." Ferron pointed in the direction he'd ridden from. "I wanted to see how long it would take for me to sell it."

"Well, let's go take a look."

Wilt got up from his desk, retrieved his hat, turned the sign hanging from the door to CLOSED, and walked outside. He then closed the door and straddled his horse, which was next to Ferron's, and Ferron also got on his horse. They started their ride out of town, and Wilt shouted over to Ferron.

"So how did your pa die?"

"We were attacked by bandits. They didn't get much, but before my pa saw them coming, he made me tuck the deed into my boot so they wouldn't get it."

"Smart man, your father was."

As they rode, they made more small talk. Ferron asked him about the town, where he could buy stock for himself and his horse, the location of a place to stay if he did not want to live on the land, and if there was a school in the area that he could possibly attend, although he had no intentions of going.

"Right yonder there's Eb's place. Name's Ebenezer, but we call him Eb for short. You can get all your supplies you need from there. Do you have money?"

"Yeah, I have a little that I scraped up along the way of getting here, doing some farm handing."

"Good, that should tide you over until we get things situated."

"O'er there is Dora Mae's place. She always has at least one bed for a stranger in town, and she cooks good too. School is on the other side of town. You won't see it the way we're going, but I can show you another time."

They put their horses into a gallop and trotted toward the property. Once they got there, Ferron and Wilt got off their horses.

As Wilt walked around the land, he came to the shack.

"That's where ya staying?"

"Yeah."

Wilt walked over to the shack and looked around. He saw the same things that Ferron had noticed when he'd arrived, although now it was a little cleaner.

"Looks comfortable enough for now."

Wilt stepped back outside with Ferron.

"You know, in order to sell this place fast, you need a well. There's no way nobody is gonna want to buy this unless you have something worthwhile."

"Do you have anyone that could dig me a well?" Ferron asked.

"Yup, have a coupla people that can do it. I'll have someone out here early tomorrow to start working on it."

Ferron was excited and felt relieved that he was going to get rid of this godforsaken land. He was also excited that Wilt had fallen for his innocent child routine. *I'll let them dig the well, let Wilt appraise it and I'll sell this land to the first pushover willing to buy it, and by the time he figures out that it's sold, I'll be long gone.*

"Well, I'll leave you be . . . unless you want to stay in town o'er Dora Mae's," Wilt said as he mounted his horse.

"No, I'll be okay here. It's not that bad, really. I've been in worse places. Besides, I have food and other provisions here."

41

"Okay, well . . . I'll have someone here for you tomorrow bright and early. His name is Herbert, and he'll do right by you. And don't worry about the cost. I'll take it out of the sale of the property."

"Thank you, sir. Thank you so much. I don't know what I woulda done if I didn't meet you."

"Don't mention it. We'll get things prepared for you so you can move on."

Wilt rode off while Ferron stood and watched him disappear into the flats.

The next morning, Ferron was awakened by a knock on the door. Startled, he wondered who would be there. Then he remembered about some guy named Herbert coming to dig a well for him. He got up from the cot in his long undergarments and opened the door. An older man with a long salt-and-pepper beard and coveralls was standing on the other side of the door.

"Hiya, lad. Name's Herbert. Wilt sent me here to dig a well for ya."

"Okay, I can help if you need me."

"No need, no need at all. You can stay in and do whatever it is you were doing. I been doing it all my life. Have it done in no time."

"Thanks." Ferron closed the door and went back to sleep.

A couple of hours later, there was loud banging on the door. It was so loud that Ferron rolled over and fell off the cot. He'd almost forgotten where he was until he looked around and saw that he was in the dilapidated shack. He got off the floor in a groggy and disgruntled mood. He wondered what was so important that this man had to be banging on his door, nearly knocking it off the rusty hinges that barely kept it in place.

"What?" Ferron said without even noticing his tone. But Herbert didn't notice either. He was too excited to notice anything except for what he needed to say.

"I was digging your well for water and . . . ," Herbert said as he jumped up and down.

"Well, yeah, that's what you are supposed to be digging."

"I was doing just that, but then something incredible happened."

Ferron finally started focusing on Herbert and noticed that he was covered in something slick and

43

black.

"Oil!" Herbert said excitedly as if it was *his* property. "Boy, we struck oil! You're rich, young man! You'll be richer than yer wildest dreams!"

Ferron looked outside and saw a one-foot geyser trickling onto the soil, coating the surrounding area like a bull's-eye on a target.

WAKING UP

Days after his last episode, Walker was sitting on a sofa inside of Dr. Steingold's office. The interior was that of a typical psychologist's office. Plaques on the wall from different universities with many specialties, awards for accomplished studies, books upon books on subjects nobody really read but which were good references in times of need. *At least the sofa is comfortable,* Walker thought, sitting opposite Dr. Steingold's desk.

"So tell me what's going on, young man." Dr. Steingold sat with his hands clasped under his chin.

"Well, as I've been telling Sheila, these . . . dreams have been wrecking my life lately," he started as his voice cracked with emotion. "I'm afraid . . . really . . .

to go to sleep for fear of having another one. It recurs whenever it wants to, and I can't stop it." As he was speaking, Walker put his head down and looked at the carpet instead of Dr. Steingold.

Steingold started writing notes on a pad while listening intently. "Okay, so you said you've been having these visions . . . uh . . . dreams since you were a child? When did they stop?"

"I don't know. Sometime after I became a teenager. I thought I was over them, but now, in the last couple of years, they just seem to be coming to me even stronger, and I don't know what to do about it anymore."

"Tell me about your last episode."

"The last time was a few days ago, when I was in the men's room at work. I saw the inside of this strange house, with this old man in my dream walking around. The old man turned toward me, and then I blacked out."

Dr. Steingold got up with his pad and pen and sat in a chair opposite Walker.

"Walker, I want to try something with you." He paused. "I want to place you under hypnosis to see if we can figure out where these dreams are derived from."

Walker looked at him distrustfully. "I don't know, Doc. I'm kinda apprehensive when it comes to that. I just came to talk and see what we can figure out."

Dr. Steingold leaned a little closer to Walker, but not enough to invade his personal space. "Have you ever heard of past-life regression?"

"Uh . . . no," he said.

"Well, what you seem to be experiencing are episodes of a past life that you may or may not be aware of. Your episodes exemplify that thought, and the only way we will be able to confirm this theory is to do what we call past-life regression on you. Now, with that said, we will record the session so we can verify our findings and have an official record of the events."

Walker was still hesitant. "But what if it doesn't give us what we are looking for? I mean . . . I don't want to get myself into a situation where something goes wrong, and I end up in an institution."

Dr. Steingold looked at Walker assuredly. "We take all precautions we have available to us, and if for any reason I see you're in danger, I'll bring you out immediately. Safely, but immediately."

Walker looked down and was still hesitant. "Okay, let's give it a try."

Moments later, Walker was lying in the kind of chic reclining chair that, strangely, you seemed to find only in a psychologist's office. He was in a hypnotic state with his eyes closed. The doctor was talking to Walker in a calm and steady voice.

"What do you see?"

Walker flashed back to 1891 onto a lake in the early evening. A young boy was sitting inside a rowboat by himself in the water. A man in another boat was moving closer to the boy.

"I'm a little boy in the middle of some water on a rowboat." Walker pauses. "A man is coming out to get me, but I have no idea of how I got there and why I am sitting in the water in the middle of nowhere."

Walker continued to hear Dr. Steingold's voice asking him questions.

"What's your name?"

Walker continued, "The little boy is in the boat with the man, heading back toward the shore with the rowboat in tow. I feel a sudden sadness . . . like I lost someone . . . close."

In a steady voice, the doctor asked Walker again. "What's your name, lad?"

"Ferron . . . Ferron Hutchers."

"Do you know where you are?"

Walker's eyes moved rapidly under his eyelids. "I'm on a shoreline."

"Where is the shoreline?"

"Connecticut. New London, Connecticut."

Walker was still lying on the recliner, with the doctor sitting in a chair next to him.

Dr. Steingold continued, "Now, I want you to go forward. To when you are a little older. What do you see?"

Walker smiled, then frowned. "I see . . . a man with me. We're . . . friends. I'm alone . . . again. Oil . . . coming . . . from the ground."

The doctor sat forward, listening more intently.

"Go further."

"I'm in a boardroom . . . of some sort. Looks like I'm . . . raging mad and screaming at the people in the room."

"Further."

"I see . . . a big house . . . mansion . . . estate. I'm . . . looking in the mirror. I'm . . . a lot older."

Walker exclaimed excitedly: "I'm the old man!"

Dr. Steingold jumped, startled by Walker's reaction. "What's happening?"

"I'm going up some stairs . . . holding a candelabra. The pain . . . in my chest! I'm trying to hold the rail . . . lost my balance."

Walker thrashed around on the recliner as though he was in pain and couldn't control his movements. "The *fire* around me . . . oh God! I'm burning! Help! I can't . . . arrrrgggghhhh!"

Dr. Steingold spoke in a controlled voice, "Walker, I will now awaken you, and all that you're experiencing will be gone. Three . . . two . . . one."

With a double finger snap from Dr. Steingold, Walker suddenly awakened, his body soaked with sweat. He looked around and tried to jump out of the recliner, as though he didn't remember where he was.

"Wh . . . what's going on? Where am I?"

The doctor took a steady hand and placed it on Walker's shoulder to try calming him down. "You're in my office. Relax. You're safe. What do you remember?"

Walker lay back down, with his hands covering his face. "I remember feeling like I was somebody else. Like I was transformed into another time and place."

Dr. Steingold looked at him with a serious expression. "Well, I need to say this, and I know it may be a shock to you, but you were someone else in the past."

Walker put his hands down and stared at the doctor. "Wait! So, you're telling me what?"

"What I'm trying to say is, the dreams that you're experiencing are actually not dreams. They are footprints of your former self in a past life."

Walker looked confused and was trying to comprehend what he was hearing. "I'm not following you, Doc."

"You see, in theory, someone dies. Sometimes the soul passes on to another person and is reborn. This has happened in your case. In a former life, you were someone named Ferron Hutchers."

Astonishment plastered Walker's face. "I don't believe you!"

Dr. Steingold talked as calmly as if he were ordering his breakfast. "Most people don't. That is why we record the session, so we can go back and analyze it with you."

"So, you mean to tell me these dreams have been trying to tell me that I was someone else before? That I was here . . . before?"

"Precisely. Now you have some avenues you need to explore. You can either let this go and hope that the dreams will cease again, or you can do some research, find out more about this person, and see why this dilemma is persistent."

Walker got up from the recliner. Dr. Steingold followed suit and rose as well. "I need to get this figured out so I can get on with my life. I'm starting to feel more and more like a prisoner to these dreams and visions."

Dr. Steingold handed Walker a copy of his recording on a flash drive.

"Well, Mr. Preston, the next step I would suggest is to take this and do some research. I would start looking in Connecticut, because that's what you mentioned while you were in your session."

Walker put out his hand to shake the doctor's. "Thanks, Doctor. When I was recommended to see you, I didn't think I would get much out of it, but now I'm kinda glad that I came."

Dr. Steingold accepted the invite and shook Walker's hand. "Well, if you have any other questions . . . or episodes that you want me to examine, feel free to call me anytime."

"I'll do that. Thanks again."

Dr. Steingold nodded and waved as Walker left his office.

WEALTH & GREED

Ferron knew nothing about the oil business, but he knew how to be shrewd. Since Herbert had been there when the oil was found, he hired him immediately. Not because he wanted to, but because he had to. Ferron knew he needed a front man for his business dealings, because no one would want to deal with a little boy, no matter how rich he was about to become.

"Herbert," Ferron said. "I know this all just happened, but how would you like to work for me?"

Herbert stared at Ferron wide eyed. He could not believe the fortune that had just been bestowed upon him. "Of course! What would you like me to do?"

"Well, first, I would like for you to plug that hole, so we won't be losing any more money coming from the ground."

Herbert was still in shock about what was happening to him and didn't register what was just said.

"Herbert! Are you working for me or not?"

"Oh, yeah . . . sure thing! I have something with me that I can use to stop that. But what about Mr. Bourg? Don't he got something to say about all this?" Herbert pointed to the hole that was oozing the black gold.

"He has nothing to do with this. I still own the land; you now work for me. So there's no need for me to give him payment for *your* work."

Herbert started getting something to temporarily plug the hole until he could get the proper equipment out there. "I see, but he's gonna be sore!"

"I don't care! Let him! What do we need him for?"

"Well, for a proper land survey, for one thing."

Ferron looked Herbert in the eyes and said, "We can hire someone else to survey. He was planning on swindling me anyway, just like I planned on swindling him."

Herbert realized he was not dealing with an boy. "Yer wiser and more clever beyond your years."

Ferron looked at him and smirked. "You have no idea."

By the end of two months, everyone in town knew who Ferron Hutchers was. After all, he was not only the richest person in town, but in the state. He was also the youngest. News spread fast about how fate had drawn him the lucky straw. Everyone wanted to be his friend and to be associated with him. He kept them all at bay. From his training with McRoss, he knew how to read every person that came toward him. He knew exactly what they wanted and how to get what he wanted from them without them realizing he had the upper hand until it was too late. He did not cheat anyone. He gave everyone their fair share of what they were looking for, but he always made sure he came out on top. *Always.*

He had people begging to survey and drill, but they wanted to pay him mere pennies. Instead, he asked questions from everyone who came to see him. He played on their emotions just so he could get the information he needed to succeed, and then he sent them on their way. He did, however, make a deal with the bank for an advancement, because, after all,

"Aren't you the only bank in town, and wouldn't you like to benefit from the spoils of the earth instead of me going someplace else?"

Soon, with the advancement and the information that he learned from those who visited, he was able to purchase the right equipment and hire the right people to do the job everyone else begged to let them do. Before they knew it, he was up and running and had all the profits to himself. Herbert didn't make out so bad either. Ferron made him an integral part of the operation and paid him well for it. Ferron was still too young for people to take seriously. But Ferron kept his own books. Nobody, not even Herbert, knew how much he was amassing from his newly found commodity.

Within a year, that old shack was removed and replaced with a small house, which was where he stayed so he could watch over his product. He trusted no one. McRoss had made sure of that. Soon Ferron began branching out by buying and creating businesses. He even beat the bank that gave him the loan at their own game and started his own. He undercut them with lower-interest loans than what they were providing. If they lowered theirs to match him, he would lower his even more. Ferron didn't care. He was all about profit, and since they'd tried to cheat him when he'd first started working with them, it made the game even more enjoyable.

Word spread to different states about this young lad, barely twenty years old, who had built such a powerful corporation from pure luck. His mother's and father's families started journeying to him to see if they were able to receive some of his good fortune. In their minds they were, after all, family. They hoped he would forgive them for not taking him in, but they had no choice because they were destitute themselves.

First an aunt came from his mother's side. She said she needed money because she was on the streets. Like his father, her husband had left her with all the kids, and she had nowhere to turn. This put a soft spot in his heart, because he knew how that felt. To be a kid with no one to depend on. Surely, he didn't want to see his cousins go through the same thing. It wasn't their fault that their parents could not take him in. So after listening to her story, he invited her into his home and let her stay until she was rested enough to make the homeward journey. He gave her more than enough to carry her and his cousins through the year. It felt good for him to help someone in need, despite all that had happened to him.

I mean, look at me now, he thought. *I have a want for nothing, and I have more than enough to spare.*

Next came an uncle on his father's side. His story was that he'd lost his job. Things were getting scarce, and he had nowhere else to turn. He was sorry that he could not have taken Ferron in, but what was he supposed to do? It had been a struggle feeding those he'd had in the house at the time, and they had been nearly starving then. This was another story that got to Ferron. He knew how it was to not have enough to eat and remembered the days and nights they suffered with no food. Ferron offered his uncle a job at one of his many businesses, but he declined because it was too far from his family, and he needed to get back to them so he could care for them. So Ferron also gave him more than enough to last throughout the year.

As time passed, he did not hear anything from his family anymore. So he hired a private detective to investigate. The news he received threw him into a fit of rage. The money he'd given them had not gone to helping their children. Instead, it had been used to buy themselves lavish gifts and furs. No food for the children, as they'd said. He also found out the two who came to see him had played a ruse on him. They were secretly lovers and had used the rest of the money to run away together, leaving their families to fend for themselves.

Ferron had had enough. He vowed from that day forward no one would ever get anything from him again. If it did not turn a profit for him, it would not be funded. All family members were cut off ... permanently! As he thought about how he had been used again, his heart grew blacker and colder. "Nothing will ever be able to penetrate my emotions again!" he vowed.

Ferron became a ferocious businessperson. The older he became, the more cantankerous. When he walked in the room, people were literally shaking in fear of his presence. Even though most businesses had failed during the Wall Street Crash of 1929, Ferron had more than enough to sustain his business endeavors, and because of that, he paid everyone handsomely. But if you didn't exceed his expectations—not meet, but exceed—you could find yourself waiting in the soup line for your next meal. You never knew when he would show up, so you had better be on your Ps and Qs when he arrived; otherwise you might be cleaning out your desk in a matter of minutes. He didn't depend on anyone, not even to fire you. Nope. He would walk to your desk or office and physically throw you out himself. He was powerful, and he knew it. No one knew how he did it, but he knew everything that was going on in all his businesses. From whom tried to take a dollar out of one of his tills to what everyone did when they were not there. It was rumored that he had a team of private detectives watching over everything and everyone . . . and a team watching *that* team.

With power and money to burn came extravagance and oddness. He bought the biggest property in Bartlesville. Just to spite the original landowners, he tore down the house that was there and built a newer and bigger one to his specifications. There was nothing wrong with the original house. He did it just so the old owners could never come back and reminisce on memories for a house that was no longer there. He even did an extensive and exhausting search for a butler whom he could "try" to eventually trust to take care of his estate when he was traveling. He settled upon a young butler from Austria who came from a family line of butlers. Since he'd just graduated from the academy, he had not worked for anyone yet, so he hadn't been corrupted, and Ferron could train him as he pleased.

Ferron loved to travel. It came from when he was with McRoss, going to many parts of the country and doing as they pleased. He'd seen so many wonders and wanted to explore even more. Now that he had the money to do it, he ventured to other countries, tried different cultures, and experimented with different belief systems.

Once, he visited East Asia and learned about reincarnation. This belief caught his eye, and he was hungry to learn more about it. He traveled to many parts of South and East Asia and India to gather as much information as he could. He was fascinated by it and became obsessed. Ferron dedicated one room as a library for anything about reincarnation, past lives, and rebirth. Although it was also part of the big picture, he didn't care much about the karma part of it. People reaping what they sowed and being nice was something he found was a weakness.

Whenever Ferron was home and not dealing with his businesses, he would read everything he could about past life and reincarnation. By 1934, after Ferron read as much as he could about the subject, he got serious about it. So serious that he wanted his lawyers to place all his assets in a trust with strict specifications. Ferron placed a call to his lawyer.

"Peason and Jeffers. How may I direct your call?"

"This is Mr. Hutchers. I want to speak to Mr. Peason."

"I'm sorry, sir, but Mr. Peason is in a meeting."

Ferron was annoyed. "Well, get him out of it! Don't you know who I am? Get him on the phone or you'll be fired before this call ends!"

The distraught switchboard operator was shaken. "Yes, sir, right away. I'll get him right now."

Ferron smiled because he knew he could do whatever he wanted to anyone, and no consequences would come his way.

"This is Peason. What can I do for you, Mr.

Hutchers?"

"You can start by firing that incompetent soul that answered the phone!"

"Sorry, Mr. Hutchers, but she's new. First day and all. She had no idea who you were."

"Well, I think she needs some formal education about who I am. I did give you the seed money to start that firm, after all."

Peason paused so Ferron could calm down a little.

"What can I do for you, sir?"

Ferron also waited, the silence deafening and awkward.

"I want you to draft me some trust papers for all my assets. My house, my companies, stocks, cash . . . all of it."

"Okay, sir, that's not a problem. Do you know who the beneficiary of the trust will be?"

"It'll be me."

Peason paused. "But sir, that's not the way . . ."

Ferron interrupted him. "I know that's not the way it works! Look, I'll be there tomorrow to explain to you specifically what I want."

"Okay, sir."

"I'll see you tomorrow at nine a.m. sharp."

"Okay, good day to you." Both Ferron and Peason hung up.

REVELATIONS/PREPARATIONS

It was late by the time Walker got home, so he decided to call it a night. Although he was restless, he slept a little more soundly than he had previously. But out of nowhere, he woke up. This time, there was no dream. Instead, there was a little boy standing at the foot of his bed. He had the saddest face on a child that Walker had ever seen. He had on overalls and a tannish shirt underneath. Walker was frozen. He could not move even if he wanted to.

The boy walked toward him with his hand extended. Objects glowed in the boy's palm, but Walker could not make out what they were. As the young boy drew closer, Walker couldn't do anything but stare. The boy placed the objects next to Walker on the bed.

The objects shined and lit up the room in a golden hue. Walker attempted to touch them, but the boy quickly grabbed them and disappeared. An impression of the objects was left on his sheets. As the golden hue dissipated, Walker was able to see the shape of three rocks. He couldn't figure out what this meant. All he knew was that this was too real for his comfort level. He went to his linen closet, pulled out sheets and a blanket, and proceeded into the living room to sleep on the couch for the rest of the night.

Walker got up in the morning, feeling weird but strangely refreshed. "The visit," as he called it, was more intriguing than it was frightening. He sensed a familiarity with the boy from last night. He wondered what the message was more than how it had happened. Since his visit to Dr. Steingold, his interest was piqued, and he wanted to get to the bottom of what was going on. As he dressed for work, he looked where the little boy had been standing last night and noticed there was still a slight golden hue on his bed where the objects had been placed. He touched the spot, but as soon as he did, he felt a slight tingle in his fingers, and the hue disappeared.

Walker arrived to work at the same time as normal. He quietly walked in and nodded to a few people. He closed his door and put the blinds down so he would not be disturbed. He still had a deadline to meet. *Funny word,* deadline, he thought. As time ticked the day away, he stayed to himself. He even ignored the couple of calls from Sheila. He wasn't ready to talk or explain what he had learned. He still had research to do and wanted to have some answers before he spoke to anyone. Especially after what had happened last night. Walker just wanted to focus on his project so he would not fall behind. He was already a day and a half overdue on his personal goal.

Before he knew it, it was 9:00 p.m. Walker had stayed longer than he'd thought or wanted to, but he had gotten a lot accomplished. He had a chance to talk with his clients and tweaked some variables that were satisfactory to all parties. He was able to proof his analysis reports and even had time to bring his manager up to speed, and he received an early congratulations for getting ahead of the rest of the team. Now it was time to go home.

After having dinner and a couple of glasses of wine, Walker was sitting at his computer. He had many tabs open on his monitor with search results from *New London, Connecticut, Ferron Hutchers*, and various articles he'd found on the man. One article interested Walker the most. It was from a newspaper article out of Oklahoma, dated July 1958. The article was about the death of Ferron Hutchers. Walker looked at the article, startled.

"This man died the same as the old man in my dream!"

As he read more of the article, he learned Ferron was very wealthy. Walker also read that the old man was heavily into reincarnation.

Walker read out loud:

"He is survived by many estranged relatives. Mr. Hutchers's will is due to be read at the law offices of Peason and Jeffers, LLC."

Walker searched and came upon more articles written about Ferron Hutchers. He continued to read aloud:

"The will is being contested by Mr. Hutchers's estranged family based on a wild delusion. Although

he had no ties to the family and they anticipated the will to be awkward, they were surprised, shocked and outraged that Mr. Hutchers left his estate to . . . 'Mr. Hutchers's newly identifiable reincarnated person.' The family argued that there is no such thing as reincarnation, so the will should not be honored. The lawyers for Mr. Hutchers stated that he was of sound mind when the will was created, and therefore it was valid. Mr. Peason of Peason and Jeffers, LLC, based in Bartlesville, Oklahoma, said Mr. Hutchers drew up a set of clues that need to be solved as proof of his reincarnated existence as a condition of the will's execution."

Walker sat back in his chair, bewildered. He reached for his phone and called Sheila.

Sheila answered the phone with sleep in her voice. "Hello?"

"Hey, it's me."

"Oh. Hey, Walk. What's going on?"

"I need to go to Oklahoma."

"Why?"

"Well, I went to your Dr. Steingold the other day, and he told me some interesting things."

"Like what?"

Walker sighed and hesitated, then spoke: "Well, he told me I was this man in a past life named Ferron Hutchers."

Sheila sat up in bed.

Walker continued, "I did some research and found out there actually was a man with the same name who died in Oklahoma. He was wealthy and left his estate to himself. The only thing is that he left it to himself when he is *reborn*! Reincarnated, so to speak. I need to go to Oklahoma and find out more. There's a law firm there that I need to go visit to get some more information."

Sheila hesitated before asking, "Would you like for me to go with you?"

Walker did not want to do this by himself, and he answered excitedly. "That would be great. Since I don't know what's going to happen, it'll be good to have someone there with me."

"When are you going?"

"I would like to go next Tuesday."

Walker waited, and then Sheila answered. "Okay. I'll be ready."

Walker smiled. "Thanks, you're always there for me."

"Hey, what are ex-girlfriends for? I'll talk with you tomorrow."

***

In bed, Sheila was sitting up, wide awake from the news she'd just received.

"Bye. We'll talk tomorrow."

Sheila punched the "Off" button on the phone and stared into space. She dialed a number and listened while it rang.

"Hi, Mom. Yeah, it's me. Something strange just happened."

***

Ferron was in Mr. Peason's office at 9:00 a.m. sharp, as promised. Mr. Peason was already sitting at his desk, waiting for his arrival. "I need you to clear your calendar for the day. We have a lot of work to do, and we can't have any interruptions."

"Okay, Ferron. What do you have for me? I understand you want to prepare your will and trust?"

"Yes, but it's going to be pretty unorthodox.

Something like this has never been done before, so we need to make sure that everything's airtight."

"Right. As I understand it, you want to do a trust for yourself . . . to yourself?"

"That's right."

Peason looked perplexed. This was something that had never been done before, but he was always up for a challenge. "Well, let us get started. I took the privilege of starting the necessary documents."

"I'm going to amend some of that, and before we get started, I'm expecting someone else to be here for another part of this process," Ferron explained. After he said this, there was a knock on the door. Peason's secretary was standing in the doorway.

"Sorry to disturb you, but there's a Dr. Neal Simmons here. I know you said you didn't want to be disturbed, but he says he's here to see you and Mr. Hutchers."

Ferron spoke before Peason could respond, "Yes, yes! Send him in!"

Peason's secretary left the doorway and reappeared with a man in his late forties, carrying a briefcase.

"Hello, Mr. Hutchers. I'm here as you directed."

"Good, good. Dr. Simmons, this is my lawyer, Jerrod Peason. Mr. Peason, this is Dr. Simmons. He's going to evaluate my mental acuity to determine that I am sane as we prepare for this process."

"How are you, sir?" Dr. Simmons put his briefcase down and extended his hand to Peason.

"I'm well. Nice to meet you, sir." Peason accepted Simmons's hand and shook it; then Simmons turned to Hutchers, "I see you're covering all your bases, Ferron. Smart move."

"Yes, I want to make sure that no one has the ability to contest my wishes."

This was Dr. Simmons's cue to begin. "Gentlemen, I'm going to ask Mr. Hutchers a series of questions and perform a battery of tests to prove his sanity and that he is of sound mind for processing the documents he wants you to prepare for him. We will need a witness to this fact so Mr. Peason will not be compromised if and when things are contested."

Peason picked up the phone and called the switchboard. "Get me Don Canton, please." After a moment, he added, "Don, could you come in here, please?"

Don Canton, a junior attorney, had started at the firm six months before, and although he had not worked on anything big yet, he was probably hoping that his opportunity had arrived.

Don entered Peason's office.

"Yes, Mr. Peason? I'm here. What can I do for you?"

"Don, this is Ferron Hutchers. I'm sure you've heard of him."

Don walked excitedly to Ferron to shake his hand. "Yes, yes I have! How do you do, sir? It's a pleasure to meet you."

"I'm fine."

"And this is Dr. Neal Simmons. He's here to evaluate Mr. Hutchers, and I need you here as a witness to attest to the fact."

"Sure! Anything to help!"

"Well, let's begin," said Dr. Simmons. "Mr. Hutchers, if I can have you take a seat here."

Ferron sat down in the chair as directed.

Dr. Simmons sat in a chair opposite Ferron. "I'll be asking you several questions about orientation to time, place, and person, and your memory. I will also be checking on your verbal and mathematical abilities, judgment, and reasoning. Mr. Canton is here to be a witness and will sign the necessary documentation to attest that he was here."

"Okay, let's get on with it." Ferron looked at Mr. Canton. "How long have you been with the firm, boy?"

"I . . . um . . . started six months ago."

Ferron liked to make people squirm. It was all in fun with him, but to others it could be a terrifying experience. "Well, stick around. You might learn something."

Dr. Simmons began his battery of tests, and Ferron answered each one with precision. His memory was as vivid as a ten-year-old's.

"Where were you born?"

"New London, Connecticut."

"Do you have family?"

"Not anymore."

"Where are you at this moment?"

"I'm at my lawyer's office of Peason and Jeffers. My lawyer, Mr. Jerrod Peason, is in the room with me, along with you, Dr. Simmons, and attorney Don Canton, who's acting as a witness."

"Good, good, Mr. Hutchers."

Dr. Simmons then gave Ferron some verbal wordplay and a test of mathematics. Ferron was clever and had always been good with numbers, so this was a breeze. Finally the doctor gave Ferron a series of questions on judgment and reasoning. Ferron passed with flying colors.

After Dr. Simmons finished his tests, he referred to Mr. Peason. "Sir, as you can see, Mr. Hutchers is of sane and sound mind, with no signs of mental instability whatsoever. I am prepared to sign any documentation to attest to such a claim."

Because Ferron did not want a lot of people to know what he was doing, he had Peason draw up the document instead of having his legal secretary or another lawyer do it. Besides, Ferron wanted to make sure everything was airtight. After Peason finished creating the document, everyone in the office looked it over for accuracy.

To any and all parties:

We, the undersigned, hereby attest to the fact that Mr. Ferron M. Hutchers was of sound mind and body when preparing the documents for his will and trust. Furthermore, it is the consensus of the undersigned that all parties were present when a Mental Acuity Test was conducted by Dr. Neal Simmons. These tests were performed on and passed by Mr. Ferron M. Hutchers.

Mr. Jerrod Peason   *Ferron M. Hutchers*
Attorney at Law   *Patient*

Dr. Neal Simmons   *Don Canton*
Doctor of Psychiatry   *Witness/Attorney*

Ferron did not want to take any chances. If Peason notarized the document, it could be thrown out as evidence to the facts for what Ferron was trying to achieve. "Could you have another attorney notarize this? Just to be on the safe side."

Mr. Peason called in another attorney to notarize the document. The notary lawyer came in, then read and checked the document. After he was satisfied that everything was correct, he gave the okay for everyone to sign it; then he placed his seal on the document. After he left, Dr. Simmons placed all his belongings in his briefcase and prepared to leave.

"Well, sirs, it was a pleasure to meet all of you."

"Same to you, from all of us." Peason spoke so no one had to repeat the sentiment. Dr. Simmons did a slight bow, turned around, and walked out the door.

"Thank you, Don, that will be all for now."

Don shook both of their hands. "Thank you for having me in to assist. Nice to meet you, Mr. Hutchers."

"Good day, sir," Ferron said flatly as the man exited the door.

Peason started to walk toward his desk. Ferron followed. Peason had a place prepared at his desk so he and Ferron could work in the same space. Ferron began to plot out the rest of the process to Peason.

"Now, to the trust agreement. What I want to have in this trust is that when I die, I want all my assets placed into it. There will be a board set up by you, with you as the director. It has to be stated that anyone who is *not* an immediate family member of yours will not be appointed as a director of the board. The board has no power to oust, fire, or terminate said director in any way possible. I also need to have placed in the trust that all my assets would be transferred to the person that can prove claim of being me reincarnated. It should also state that the person will have to answer four out of twenty random questions . . . clues, if you will . . . which I will give you during the course of time, and that only I would know the answers to. Once they have done that, it will be proof that it is I. Any claims of being my immediate family are false. I do not have any children or plan to in the near future. Should that change, all documents would be amended immediately to reflect such a change. Only you or a trusted child of yours will have access to the documents and the clues. I also have two letters, one to be placed with the clues and the other to be opened only by the reincarnated me once everything has been finalized."

As Ferron spoke, Peason was jotting down everything to make sure he did not miss anything. He began drafting the documents, proofed them, and did a couple of amendments for the final documents. He looked them over once more and gave the documents to Ferron for approval. Ferron was satisfied, and the final stages to complete his wishes went into effect.

After signing the documents, Ferron had other business to complete with Peason. He kept tabs on everyone whom he employed, even those close to him. He did not care what the outcome was, but if he got wind of something that was amiss, he dealt with it swiftly and without remorse. "Do you have the information that I asked you about?"

Peason opened his top desk drawer and pulled out an envelope addressed to Ferron. He placed it on his desk and slid it to Ferron. "I didn't open it as you requested, but here it is. I got it last night."

Ferron opened it and smirked. *Just as I thought,* he said to himself.

"I hope it's good news, sir." Peason was intrigued with what Ferron was looking at.

"It is for me, but not for someone else," Ferron noted as he placed the contents back into the envelope and put it into his briefcase. He stood up and started to leave. "You'll hear about the contents of this package soon enough."

As Ferron walked out the door, he bid Peason farewell and headed downstairs to his waiting car.

CONVINCING

The following Tuesday, Walker and Sheila caught the 6:15 a.m. flight out of Newark Airport to get to Bartlesville, Oklahoma. But first they needed to make the forty-five minute to an hour drive from Tulsa Airport. By noon, they were standing outside the corporate office of Peason and Jeffers. They walked into the building and took the elevator to the law office's main floor.

Walker and Sheila were alone and standing beside each other in the elevator.

Sheila turned to Walker. "Are you nervous?"

"Yeah. I'm not sure what I'm getting myself into being here."

Sheila took Walker's hand and squeezed it. "Well, I'm glad I'm here with you. I'm just as curious as you are to find out more about this."

Walker looked Sheila in her eyes. "I am too."

They began to kiss, but the elevator doors opened. They walked off the elevator together and toward the receptionist, who was sitting behind a large mahogany desk with the signage of PEASON AND JEFFERS, LLC, embroidered in gold letters on the wall behind her. The receptionist was busy answering calls and stopped to acknowledge Walker and Sheila.

"Hello, welcome to Peason and Jeffers. May I help you?"

"Yes, my name is Walker Preston, and I'm here to see Mr. Peason."

"Do you have an appointment?"

"No."

"I'm sorry, Mr. Preston, but he doesn't see anyone unless you have an appointment. If you'd like, you can . . ."

Walker interrupted her. "It's concerning Mr. Hutchers."

The receptionist was surprised but kept her composure.

"Did you say . . . Mr. Hutchers?"

"Yes. Ferron Hutchers."

The receptionist became livelier, the day suddenly interesting.

"Hold on."

The receptionist picked up the phone and talked low so Walker and Sheila were not able to hear her. After a brief conversation, she hung up the phone.

"Mr. Peason will be right out."

Walker and Sheila sat in the lobby. Moments later, a man in his mid-forties walked into the lobby and approached the pair.

"Mr. Preston?"

Peason was dignified from the ground up: impeccably dressed, complete with matching tie and kerchief.

Walker got up from the chair, approached Mr. Peason, and extended his hand to shake Peason's.

"Yes, and this is my friend Sheila. How are you?"

"I'm well. Would you two follow me to my office, please?"

Walker and Sheila trailed Mr. Peason to his office. It was not only huge, but as immaculate as he was dressed. The shiny varnished oak desk looked like something that was taken from the 1930s, but it was so well maintained it might have been bought yesterday. They sat in two chairs opposite Mr. Peason's desk.

Peason had a look of caution.

"I understand you have some information about Mr. Hutchers."

Walker looked him straight in his eyes with all the belief he could muster, even though it still seemed surreal to him.

"Yes. I believe I'm Mr. Hutchers."

Peason sat up in his chair and looked at Walker, then Sheila. "What makes you think you're Hutchers?"

"Well, I've been having these dreams of an old man since I was a kid. The dream was of him dying in a fire."

Peason looked at him woodenly.

"My great-grandfather was Mr. Hutchers's lawyer. Many people over the years have come in and said they were him. We even had a lady come in and say that her eight-year-old daughter was this guy. But no one was able to really *prove* they were Ferron Hutchers. Besides, most people have recurring dreams."

Sheila chimed in: "Yes, but not like this. I mean, sometimes he'll wake up and act like he's on fire."

Peason wasn't convinced. "That doesn't prove any—"

Walker jumped in before he could finish. "Look, I don't mean to sound critical, but I've dealt with this all my life. I thought I was going crazy until this." Walker took out a flash drive and eyed a device on Peason's desk to connect it to. "May I?"

Peason was still skeptical, but said, "By all means. Knock yourself out."

Walker placed the flash drive into the device and played the recorded session from Dr. Steingold. Peason listened to it intently. When the recording finished, Peason sat back in his chair with his hands behind his head, then reseated himself in a more professional manner. He looked at Sheila, then to Walker.

"This doesn't prove anything to me. The recording could be an elaborate scheme to make a claim. Like I said earlier, many people have come here to stake the execution of Mr. Hutchers's will."

"He gave him a bag of pyrite for three gold nuggets," Walker blurted out.

Peason tried to stay stoic, but this startled him. "What did you say?"

"I . . . I mean Ferron gave the traveling salesperson a bag . . . er . . . pouch of pyrite for three gold nuggets."

Peason looked at Walker, astonished.

"How did you know about that? Where did you get that information?" Peason asked in an accusatorial tone.

Walker looked down because he felt embarrassed with everyone staring at him. "It's something I picked up during my dreams."

Walker realized the little boy who had appeared in his room was trying to give him a clue. *That was Ferron!* Now it made sense. The glowing objects were the nuggets he'd traded.

Peason got up from his desk and walked to the other end of the large room. He bent down and opened the doors of a bureau that looked just as old and pristine as his desk. Behind the doors was a wooden panel. He slid it open and unveiled a safe.

As Mr. Peason dialed in the combination to open the safe, he explained, "Mr. Hutchers had this built for my great-grandfather a long time ago. It was made specifically to hold Mr. Hutchers's will, instructions, and clues with the answers to them. You, my friend, just answered one of those clues. No one except for Ferron and the bagman would have known that info, and I'm quite sure the bagman wouldn't have said anything to anyone, because he'd gotten duped by a boy."

After he opened the safe, he pulled out some documents, two envelopes, and an old manila folder. "These documents you see here are the trust that was set up by Ferron Hutchers and drafted by my great-grandfather. One envelope contains the clues Mr. Hutchers created for anyone who claimed to be him. The other holds the answers to those clues that will be able to positively identify that person as the newly reincarnated Ferron Hutchers. Like I said earlier, no one has been able to answer all these questions. Some have come close, but answering all four has proved impossible. There are a total of twenty clues that are randomly changed every time someone makes a claim, but only four of those twenty that have been selected and put into the envelope must be answered. My descendants personally made the changes, and now it has been bestowed upon me to be the charge for this duty."

Walker and Sheila hung on every word Mr. Peason was saying.

"I do have the responsibility to tell you that his estranged family has been in a fight for a long time to contest the will and trust. Luckily for us, Mr. Hutchers was very astute. Because of the peculiar nature of his trust, he was evaluated by a psychiatrist and was deemed to have a sound mind and all his mental faculties. Included in these documents is a notarized statement attesting to the fact. So the family has been fighting an uphill battle with this for decades."

"What did he leave behind?" Walker asked.

"Too much to mention, but everything is in the documents and trust that are here. I really don't want to go into detail about it, not until everything is proved."

Walker's head was spinning. He wondered what he had gotten himself into. What were the chances that this was really happening? Although he was hanging on every word Mr. Peason was saying, he started daydreaming of the possibilities of being the man who had invaded his dreams all these years.

"What happened to the estate, the companies?" Sheila asked.

"They are still being managed by the board. I'm the director of the board, so everything has been running smoothly."

"Could you at least tell me how much it is all worth, since I did get one of the random clues correct?"

Peason pondered, then said, "That's fair. At the last quarterly meeting, it was estimated that the trust was worth about forty billion dollars."

Walker couldn't help but wonder what he would do with all that cash. "May I see those clues?" Walker asked Peason.

"Sure." As he handed Walker one of the envelopes, he explained, "You don't have to answer them right away. Like I said, many have tried, but all have failed.

Once you think you have the answers, come see me, and we'll open the second envelope together, here in my office."

Walker studied the envelope that Peason had given him. "Okay, but I really don't know how or if I want to embark on this journey."

"It's your choice, Mr. Preston. I think you should, because you never know. If you're able to answer the clues, your world will most certainly change. But if you can't—no harm, no foul."

Walker took the envelope and extended his hand again to Mr. Peason. "Thank you for all this. I really appreciate it."

"No, thank you. You made this an interesting morning for me. But now if you'll excuse me, I'm due in court in a couple of hours, and I need to prepare."

Walker and Sheila left the office and went to the elevator. Once in, Sheila showed her excitement. "Walker! Did you hear that? Do you know what this could possibly mean? Imagine if you find out that you're really this guy?"

But Walker was in his own world. Sheila's voice sounded like bass drumbeats running in his head.

"Walker? Why aren't you answering me?"

"Oh, sorry, I was just thinking about the possibilities. I'm kinda scared and don't really want to explore it, but like he said, what do I have to lose?"

"Sounds to me like you have a lot to gain."

"Yeah, you're right. But I'm also worried about that family that has been fighting this all these years. What'll happen if this is true?"

Sheila was quiet for a few moments, then said, "Walker, I have something to tell you, but it can wait until we get back to the hotel."

"You can tell me now; it's okay."

"No," Sheila said quietly. "I think I'll wait until then."

"Okay, that's fine since I have a lot to think about right now."

***

They finally arrived at their room after checking in. They both put their bags down. Walker went to the suite's bar to get two glasses and a bottle of red wine. Sheila was already on the couch, shoes off and feet kicked up against the armrest. Walker noticed she had to be tired. They had been at it since 4:00 a.m. He set the glasses and the bottle on the coffee table and poured two glasses. He took one for himself and began to hand her one, but saw that Sheila had her eyes closed. She didn't notice he was back until he sat on the couch. She slowly opened her eyes.

"Oh, hey. I must've dozed off."

"It's okay. I can understand you being tired."

"Walker?"

"Yeah?"

"I need to tell you something. I hope when I do, you don't get upset."

"What's wrong?" Walker was puzzled about what kind of news she had to tell him.

"I never talked about it because it really didn't matter to me. Plus I always saw it as a winless point, so I never looked at it as a big deal. Then you told me your news the other day, and it startled . . . no . . . shocked me."

"What do you mean? What are you talking about?"

"Well, remember when you were telling me about Ferron Hutchers? About your session, and you figured out it was him in your dreams?"

Walker was unsure where this was going. "Ummm . . . yeah?"

"That name is part of my family's name. My mother's maiden name is Hutchers. I heard rumors of him. My mother and her sister and brothers have been fighting to get that trust revoked. Ferron Hutchers is my great-granduncle."

Walker was confused. How did he not know this about her family? They'd dated for a couple of years, and it just dawned on him that she'd never talked about them. "Wait . . . what?"

Sheila sighed. "I had no clue about any of this. When you told me what happened at Dr. Steingold's office and told me Hutchers's name, I was in disbelief. Then after going to the lawyer's office with you and hearing everything that was said, I was in total shock." She took her feet off the couch to sit down next to Walker.

"I could've never imagined that this would ever happen, let alone through someone I know. My family would have never thought any of this would be possible. That's why they fought so hard to contest the trust."

Walker turned to her. "What about you? Where are you in all this . . . with your family?"

Sheila looked even more serious. "I never cared about it. I figured that was their fight, and I didn't want to have anything to do with it. Especially when I heard about the kind of man he was."

"What do you mean?"

"He was awful! He ran his life and business like he was the devil himself. People literally shook when he walked into a room."

Walker wanted to hear more about her family's involvement, but he didn't want to taint what he knew he had to do. He wanted to get to the bottom of all this. He wanted these dreams and visions to stop, and the only way he thought they would was to go through the process of solving these clues. "Whatever your family is going through with this has nothing to do with me. I just want to get this over with. Anything after that, I'll deal with it when it happens."

He sat back and leaned against her, exhausted. He hadn't realized how tired he was until that moment, but the familiarity of lying against her felt good. She automatically started caressing him. Something stirred between the two, and they began kissing. Walker didn't know if it was the wine, the exhaustion, or the journey they were on together. But at this moment, he didn't care. Walker whispered to her, "It's late and you're tired. I think we should get some rest before our flight in the morning." Before he could say another word, she got up and went straight to the bedroom.

Walker followed her into the bedroom, and upon seeing that she had begun discarding her clothes, he followed suit and began undressing as well. Sheila lifted the bedcover and slipped underneath. Walker got in on the opposite side and pulled her toward him.

She kissed him, and Walker started caressing her, the heat between them increasing. As if both thinking the same thing, they stopped and looked into each other's eyes, wondering if they should go further.

Human frailty and the span of time since they'd been together answered their unspoken question.

The following morning, they woke next to each other. Sheila was still sleeping soundly when Walker woke up. He thought to himself how much he'd missed her, and she'd proved that she'd missed him too. He gently nudged her and kissed her on the back of her neck. "Sheila, wake up. We need to get ready to get out of here."

Sheila stirred, then turned around to face him. A smile came across her face. "Good morning. Feels good to wake up next to you again." Neither knew where this would lead, but both were glad for where they were right now. Although they didn't want to admit it, it was long overdue.

"Same here," Walker said as he kissed her forehead, "but we need to take it slow this time, especially with what's going on." They looked into each other's eyes.

"You're right." Then Sheila got into her old joking character. "Wait, if it turns out that you're Hutchers, does that mean you're now my great-granduncle?" she said with a laugh.

Walker pondered. "Hmmm, I don't know, but at least I'll be rich."

They got up, took a shower together, and began packing so they could catch their flight.

***

Later that evening, Walker was home alone. He finally had privacy to think and process everything that had happened in the last few days. He sat at the dining room table and looked at the envelope he'd received from Mr. Peason. As he stared at the envelope, there was a fulcrum of excitement and fear that rocked his senses. Walker opened the envelope and read the letter contained inside.

To those who attempt to stake a claim to be the reincarnated persona of Ferron Hutchers, I have a series of questions that only I would know the answers to. I have always been a private person, and the questions you possess would only be answerable by me. My attorney, Mr. Peason, or his successor are the only person(s) who would be able to verify your responses as true. These questions have been randomly selected by me for the first round. However, if someone stakes claim and is not able to give the correct responses, another round of questions will be selected by my attorney or his successor. I chose this manner so no group of people can gather together to stake claim of my trust. Enclosed, you will find those clues. Each must be answered before the next step is set in motion.

Walker picked up the other piece of paper and read the questions.

1. Who was the first person I trusted that betrayed me?

2. What did I trade with the traveling salesperson?

3. Where did my butler come from, and why did I select him?

4. What happened to Herbert?

Walker remembered listening to his session and recalled having one friend besides his brother. He took the flash drive out of his briefcase and put it in the USB port of his laptop. He started listening and closed his eyes. As he listened, some of the images came into focus. A train ride came into his mind. It was so vivid that he could actually hear the clickety-clack of the train wheels banging onto the tracks. Even the scent of the boxcar wood permeated his senses. A flash came and went of a man as light slipped through the separated slats of the boxcar. As the recording continued to play in the background, Walker was transported back into a time he knew nothing about but was strangely familiar with. Sights and sounds of the present dissipated while those of the past engulfed him. Then he heard someone making fun of a name.

"F-F-Ferron, huh? That's a weird one. Why all the Fs in front of your name?" said the voice that didn't belong to him.

"Ferron, my name is Ferron," Walker heard himself say out loud. He no longer heard the recording.

"Oh, that's better, but it's still weird. The name's McRoss, Pete McRoss, but you can call me Rossy. That's what my friends call me," he heard the second voice recite.

Flashes of other images started ringing through him. Images of him and this Rossy guy traveling together and doing deals and trades flowed through his mind like someone window-shopping. He experienced the joy this person was feeling being around this guy. Learning, traveling, amassing more money than he had ever seen. The flashes began to slow. Walker saw through Ferron's eyes that he was sitting across from this man. He felt a bit of sadness as he looked at Rossy. He witnessed the hand-off of the boxes. He also saw what Ferron did not see at the moment when it happened . . . the switch that Rossy did when Ferron bent to pick up the items that were knocked down. Walker gasped as he witnessed this deceit. When Ferron opened his box and saw what he was actually left with, Walker felt the same anger and mistrust that flowed through Ferron. He was beginning to understand why Ferron had become the man he was. Those he felt close to always seemed to hurt, betray, or disappoint him. Walker felt the cold and sadness that started to envelop Ferron's heart.

Abruptly, Walker found himself back in his own reality. He was still sitting in his chair but noticed he had lost an hour. He looked around and felt different. He still felt like himself but . . . changed. Walker could not put his finger on it, but somehow his demeanor had a slight alteration. He stared around the room, then closed his eyes to try to get his bearings back. Once he felt a little more normal, Walker picked up the sheet with the clues on it and read them over. One of the clues caught his eye.

Who was the first person I trusted that betrayed me?

Walker now knew where he was being driven to and why. The answer was vividly clear to him. He knew who the person was that betrayed Ferron's trust! He opened a new document on his laptop and quickly jotted down the question and the newly found information.

Who was the first person I trusted that betrayed me?

Pete McRoss, also known as Rossy, was the one who betrayed me. We were good friends until he tricked me and changed a box with my earnings to another one. But the trick was on him. Because of his deceitfulness, he ended up making me richer than I could ever dream.

He also put the second question on here since it was already answered at the lawyer's office:

What did I trade with the traveling salesperson?

I gave the traveling salesperson a pouch of pyrite for three gold nuggets. This was during my travels to Oklahoma.

He was not sure if he would need it, but he wanted to make sure there was no question to his discovery, so he wrote down all that he could remember. Walker was tired after this ordeal. It was already getting close to midnight, and he still had to go to work tomorrow. Walker placed the papers back into the envelope, made sure the document he had just created was saved, and shut down his laptop.

Although he was tired, Walker still lay restless in bed. As he listened to the silence in his apartment, more thoughts came to mind. He could not shake the fact that after all these years, he was finally getting answers to something that had been haunting him since childhood. Never in his wildest dreams would he have thought of a conclusion like this. As he finally started to drift off, he had more questions than answers.

SELFISH MOTIVES

Ferron was pleased with how his plan had gone into effect. Now he could live his life and continue to amass his wealth without a care in the world. As he was driven back home, he watched as the people who had less than him milled about on the sidewalks. He saw families scurrying about, going to the ice-cream parlor and various stores, men with their carts selling fruits and other wares to eke out a living. Ferron was glad he wasn't one of the saps who had to do such nonsense to get by.

His life was set, and he knew it. Not only was he shrewd, but he had the natural insight to foresee what would be profitable. Because he was a supplier of oil, he knew what was going on in the new and young auto industry. So after the dust settled with everyone trying to start new automobile companies, through his various companies, he invested in the final "Big Three" to make sure he had all his bases covered should one fail, or one became more profitable than the others.

Though no one knew it, Ferron's first investment was with Henry Ford. He saw the innovative spirit in him, and it proved to be one of Ferron's best investments among those that he didn't control. As a matter of fact, the very limo he was riding in had been the first one off the assembly line. His investment package included Ferron getting the first production car of any vehicle he wanted. In 1919, when Henry Ford wanted to buy his stock back from all investors, he dared not ask Ferron about his stock options because of the deals he was getting from other products Ferron owned. Ford knew that Ferron was callous enough to choke him out of the products he needed to make his automobiles, so he thought of it as a good business decision not to negotiate but to let things be.

The other two major auto companies silently worked with the investments and knew Ferron was involved with them all, but his influx of seed money gave them the unlimited ability to compete with the others.

Ferron wanted to go to his corporate office and surprise everyone, just to see whom he could put fear into for the day. So he directed his driver to take him. He knew Herbert would be there. The driver stopped in front of the building, and while Ferron waited for him to come around and open the door, he marveled at the structure he'd built. It was small . . . only four stories tall, but he knew that was all he needed to work his empire.

As he stepped out of the car, the concierge hurried to open the main entrance door so Ferron would not have to pause. He'd witnessed Ferron berate the last concierge who hadn't opened the door soon enough and so had made Ferron wait. He was fired for a twenty-second delay. Twenty seconds! This concierge wanted to make sure there were no mistakes on his part.

"Good morning, Mr. Hutchers. I'm hoping you're having a good day," the concierge said, performing a slight bow as Ferron walked through.

"Hmmmph," Ferron grunted. "Every day is a good day when you're me!" he replied, not missing a beat.

The main floor was well furnished. It reflected the parts of the world where he had traveled. The decorator made use of everything he'd picked out and made it tasteful, although items came from all over. The floor was partially carpeted with a Spanish decor he'd picked out while traveling through Barcelona, and the tile was chosen from a small shop in Venice. The wall sitting behind the main reception area was mauve and the rest of the walls a stark white. Giant mahogany pillars stood guard against the sides of the matching desk where the receptionist and the switchboard operator shared space for their daily tasks. Vases from India and Asia with artwork from Africa and furniture from parts of the United States completed the ensemble. The big windows that hugged the entrance doors brought in enough light so that the collision of items from around the world looked like the work of an interior conductor creating a visual masterpiece.

The lift attendant eyed Ferron when he came into the building and made sure the elevator was ready, doors open. "Good morning, Mr. Hutchers." The elevator attendant gestured toward the open doors. Ferron walked in, lost in thought, and didn't bother to answer. The attendant closed the doors and took the elevator to the fourth floor, where Ferron's office and conference room were located.

As Ferron stepped off, there was a brief pause of work activity while everyone stood to greet him. Each person sat down and began working again after he passed them. He went directly into his office and picked up the phone. It was answered on the first ring.

"Have Herbert come in here," he beckoned to the operator.

"Right away, Mr. Hutchers."

Herbert came into the office and sat down. "You called for me, sir?"

"Yes. You know, you've been with me since the beginning of my endeavors."

"Yes, I have," Herbert replied.

Ferron continued, "Do you feel as if you've been compensated well for what you do for me?"

"Oh yes! Yes I do!" Herbert exclaimed excitedly.

Ferron opened his briefcase and took out an envelope. He then spread the envelope's contents on his desk like a deck of cards. It was an assortment of photographs and documents. He pretended to intensely study them; then he looked up at Herbert. "Then why did you do things that have betrayed my trust?" he said, staring coldly.

"Ferron, I have no idea what you're talking . . ."

"No, right now I'm Mr. Hutchers to you!" he screamed, picking up one of the pictures and flinging it at Herbert.

Herbert's eyes grew wide, and he tried to keep his composure. "Sir, what is this?"

"It's *you*, making deposits of *my* money for yourself! You know, embezzling!" Ferron shouted as he turned red.

"I . . . I don't understand what you're . . ."

"Oh, you don't? Well, let me elaborate." Ferron began reading one of the documents in front of him and then put it in front of Herbert. "I've been having you followed since the beginning. You were doing great and did everything you were supposed to. But somewhere along the line, you figured that I lost track of what was going on and thought you could get away with stealing from me."

Herbert stared at the pictures, baffled.

"These documents are statements from every bank you have an account with, including the Swiss ones." He then pushed a button. Moments later, two burly men opened the door and stood behind Herbert.

Ferron was now seething, talking with clenched teeth, and he stood up behind his desk. "I will be taking the liberty to have documents drawn up for you to sign. What you're going to do . . . *Herbert*, is sign those documents. That will be the authority to have *every* penny you stole from me transferred back to where it belongs, along with the interest you gained from it and any other money, stocks, and bonds you earned while working for me. To make sure you don't get any ideas of leaving town before everything is finalized, these two lovely gentlemen will be with you. I don't mean be with you at your house, but have you under lock and key in a special place I made just for situations like this. Once I have *everything* you own, then and only then will you be able to go."

After he finished, he sat down and turned his head to the side, as if to dismiss Herbert. "Get him out of my office, roughly! I want everyone to see you take him out of here in the worst way possible! I want you to make sure it is imprinted in everyone's noggin that you don't fuck with what I have!"

The two men picked up Herbert under his arms as if he were a rag doll. Once they had him lifted out of the chair, they grabbed him by the legs and carried him out of Ferron's office.

As everyone started hearing the commotion coming out of the office, they stopped working. They saw Ferron's door swing open and gasped as a wide-eyed Herbert was being carried away like a sack of potatoes, legs attempting to kick himself free. But the two men had such a grip on him that it was useless. Their grips were like vises on all his extremities. Instead of waiting for the elevator, they went to the stairwell and carried him out headfirst. The other employees looked like scared children hiding from their worst nightmares as they watched the scene unfold in front of them.

As the three approached the first floor, everyone heard the chaos and turned in the direction of the turmoil. The two men's feet slapped against the expensive Venetian tile as they headed to the door. Men and women moved out of the way, looking on in disbelief. The concierge was also in shock, but he regained his composure in enough time to open the door as the tornado steamed toward him.

A waiting car stood idling at the entrance of the building. As if on cue, the back door opened, and the two men threw Herbert into the car. Before Herbert could react, one of the men climbed into the back and closed the door, while the other sat in the front passenger seat. As the car whisked away, heads were peering through the windows on each floor. That was the last anyone ever saw of Herbert.

***

The night stole Walker's time again. He tossed and turned as he slept. Images were more vivid. Smells seemed as real in his dreams as when he was awake. Walker felt his footsteps hitting the concrete as he approached the warehouse. People milled about, doing their daily duties. Forklifts moved boxes of freight along designated but imaginary lines to parts selected for storage. Workers didn't seem to notice him as he strolled through. He even bumped into one man, but the worker just kept walking as though nothing had happened. Walker was being guided through the area. He had no idea where he was going but felt like he'd been there before.

He stopped at a door leading to stairs. While he walked down those stairs, the trip to the bottom also seemed familiar. There was a man sitting there with a long chain attached to one of his ankles. Two large-framed men kept close to him. A voice unfamiliar to Walker came from the exact place in which he stood. It appeared to be coming from him. "I hope your . . . uhmmm . . . stay has been pleasant down here." He felt the words form in his mouth, but he knew he wasn't speaking them.

"How long am I going to be here?" he heard the shackled man ask.

"You're in luck," he heard the voice coming from him say. "Everything is finalized. All that you took from me and all that you gained while you worked for me is now mine." Walker felt coldness in his heart, but it wasn't *his* heart. "I came here to release you, Herbert. But before I do, you will do exactly what I tell you. Any deviation from my instructions now or in the future shall have severe consequences for you. Do you understand?" Walker felt himself sneer, but it was as though the facial expression was being controlled by someone else. He sensed that this man had taken something from him.

"I understand," the man said with his head bowed. "I just want to get outta here!"

"When this place is empty of workers tonight," Walker heard the voice say as he pointed to the two men, "they will take you to the outskirts of this town. There you will find a car and two hundred dollars in cash. You are to leave this area and never return." Walker felt himself move closer to the man named Herbert, and he looked right into his eyes. "If I hear you are within one hundred miles from here at any time, all bets are off. You will never know what or when I'll do something, but know that I will. It will be quick. It will be swift, and you will never see it coming. Do you understand these instructions?"

He saw Herbert's eyes widen with fear, as if he knew the threat would be carried out. "Y-y-yes, I do, Mr. Hutchers. I will leave this place and never return."

Walker now knew that he was hearing, seeing, and speaking through Ferron Hutchers. His point of view turned toward the two other men in the room. "You have your instructions of what to do. Take him to the edge of town, where we placed the car, and make sure he leaves." He saw the two men look at each other and nod.

As Walker felt himself turn and head toward the steps, everything went black, and he went into a deep sleep.

Walker woke up lying on the floor by his bedroom door. He didn't remember how he got there or even getting out of bed, for that matter. He felt a little groggy as he picked himself up off the floor. His room looked different. The floor felt like concrete even though he saw carpet. His bedroom windows transformed into dingy white walls, and all his furniture disappeared right before his eyes. Support beams appeared and riddled the room as the lighting dimmed.

"What the hell . . . ?" Walker exclaimed as his view was no longer familiar to him. What did look familiar was the man he had seen last night in his dream. He saw the man getting unchained by two shadowy men.

The man, the name Herbert came to mind, was illuminated, while everything else was opaque. Walker saw the men take Herbert by the arms and lead him to the stairs that suddenly came into Walker's view. As they went up the stairs and out the door, the room darkened as the light followed them. They stepped through a hole that led them outside. Walker saw one man get behind the steering wheel while the other led Herbert to the front passenger-side door. The second man got into the back seat and they drove away. A white flash came about, and everything was normal again. His bed, windows, and floors were in place as they should be.

Disoriented from the ordeal, Walker attempted to get his wits about him. As he regained his composure, it became clear that he was being led to the answer to another question. He went into the living room and grabbed his briefcase. Walker sat on the couch, opened the envelope, and pulled out the documents that contained the questions.

What happened to Herbert?

The vivid images of his dream and the last few moments gave Walker the answer he was looking for, so Walker opened his laptop and typed in his answer to the fourth question:

Herbert was caught embezzling. He was taken to a warehouse and held in the basement but then released after he signed documents relinquishing all his assets. He was then driven out of town and told not to come back under any circumstances.

He closed the laptop, gathered his items to put back in his briefcase, went to take the hottest shower he could stand, and got ready for work.

TRANSPOSITION

Walker arrived at work at his usual time. As he walked into the building, something seemed off. The first-floor interior was changed. *How did they do a remodel that quickly?* he asked himself. Where a glass partition had stood for the security desk, a mahogany desk was sitting in its place. The interior now had walls in place of windows and different flooring. As a matter of fact, Walker *felt* different. As he strolled to the elevator, he noticed a man just . . . standing there. When he got to the elevator, the man held the door open, walked in, and pushed the button to his floor. *Never saw elevator attendants here before,* Walker thought.

Once the door opened to his floor, Walker stepped through the double glass doors and headed straight to his office. He opened his briefcase and stared into it.

Everything in it looked foreign to him. Walker picked up a slim contraption and placed it on his desk. He studied it and noticed it was sliced in two halves. He took the unhinged part of it to flip it open. It had a clear black piece of glass staring back at him, with keys on the bottom half that looked like a typewriter. *What the hell is this?* Walker thought as he examined the machine closely. Baffled, he finally closed it, pushed it aside, and opened his top desk drawer. He rummaged through it but could not find what he was looking for.

"Where in the hell is all my stuff? Paper, notebooks, ledgers?" Walker mumbled to himself. He picked up his phone, waiting for someone to answer, but all he heard was a loud, steady tone.

"What the hell is going on? Why is no one picking up this damn phone? I'll fire the lot of 'em!" he screamed. Walker stepped out of his office and bellowed, "Who in the hell's been in my office, and where are the materials that should be in my desk drawer?"

Everyone stopped and looked at Walker, then at each other with perplexed glances. Finally, a woman got up and headed toward him. "No one's been in your office, Walker. As far as your things in your top drawer, whatever you had should be in there."

"Well, they're not! And who the fuck is Walker?" he screeched. His coworkers were dumbfounded. They all just stared at him.

Finally, his manager, Mr. Reese, appeared. "What's going on here?"

The woman who'd tried to help Walker spoke up. "Um, sir. He thinks someone went into his office and took something, but his door is always locked, so no one could get in there even if they wanted to."

The manager approached Walker and put his hand on his shoulder as Walker seethed. "Son, are you okay?"

Walker was beet red with anger. "Get your fucking hand off me! Who do you think you are? I should fire you just for touching me!"

"Now see here, Walker! I don't know what's going on with you, but you better—"

Walker stopped the manager midsentence. "Like I said, who the *fuck* is Walker? I own this place, and how dare you try to give me an ultimatum?"

The manager looked aghast. As the screaming continued, Sheila and others from around the building started coming into the corridor to figure out what was happening. At this point, the manager became just as angry as Walker. "You need to watch your mouth before you find yourself fired!"

"Fire *me*? No one fires *me*! I'm Ferron Hutchers, and I own all this!" Walker exclaimed as he spread out his arms, indicating the whole area.

Sheila saw Walker was having a past-regression episode and ran between the two men so she could calm the commotion. "Mr. Reese, he hasn't been feeling well. Let me help."

Mr. Reese looked angrily at Sheila, then to Walker and back to Sheila. "You better get this handled before I handle it myself."

Sheila slid farther between them. "I will. Let me take it from here." She stood there as the manager took one last hard look at Walker. Mr. Reese turned to stroll away, mumbling, "I don't need this shit today. I got too much on my plate right now."

Sheila spun her body to face Walker. "Um, Mr. Hutchers?" Walker stared right at Sheila but didn't seem to recognize her. "Mr. Hutchers, I apologize for all this. Can we go into your office and see what I can help you with?"

"That's more like it!" Walker said. "Somebody who's not afraid to step up. Follow me into my office."

Walker turned toward his office with Sheila right behind him, and the rest of the workplace began to slowly disperse to continue their work. Once inside Walker's office, Sheila closed the door behind them. She could see some of their coworkers trying to peer into the office from their cubicles.

Sheila calmly said, "I'm sorry, Mr. Hutchers. Sometimes people forget who they are."

"Well, they need to remember me!" Walker was still angry but was starting to calm down.

"So what is it you need assistance with?"

"I can't find my files, and I got this weird-looking thing on my desk." Walker pointed to the laptop, which seemed foreign to him. Sheila walked to the desk and picked it up. She studied it as if it were the first time she'd seen something like it before. "Well, whatever it is," Sheila said as she turned it around on

123

all sides and then put it down, "it's pretty fancy. But let's not worry about it for now."

"But where are my files, notes, and ledgers? No one has access to my office. The only person who did was Herbert, and he's no longer here!"

"Are you sure you didn't take them home?" Sheila was trying to steer him in another direction until his episode was over.

"No! Because if I did, they would've been in my briefcase!"

"Why don't you have a seat, sir, and relax while I look around for you. Let me handle your affairs for the day."

Walker looked at her suspiciously. "How are you going to handle my affairs? Do you even know what I'm doing right now?"

Sheila thought for a moment, then smiled. "Mr. Hutchers, you can relax right here." She directed him to a chair located away from the desk. "I'm sure you have a lot to do for the day, but just relax for a few minutes and close your eyes so things can calm down within you. Maybe you'll remember where you last saw the items you're looking for."

Walker sat in the chair, leaned back, and closed his eyes. Sheila stood guard as Walker appeared to fall asleep. Time eroded as she watched. Ten minutes later, Walker awakened. He looked confused. "Hey, Sheila."

"Hey, Walker."

He held his head as if he had a bad headache. "How did I get here? Where did you come from?"

Sheila went to him and put her hand on his shoulder. "Welcome back."

"Welcome back? What do you mean?"

"Well, somehow you came here and started ranting. You caused quite a stir with a lot of commotion."

"Huh? How?" Walker looked puzzled. "I don't understand."

"Dude, you don't remember anything?"

Walker was rubbing the back of his neck. "Ummm, no."

Sheila pulled up another chair to sit opposite Walker, face-to-face. "You came in here as Mr. Hutchers. Said you were looking for some items and thought someone came into your office and took them."

His eyes grew as big as saucers. "Really?"

"Yup. You even had a verbal fight with Mr. Reese. You both were talking about firing each other. You told him you owned the place. I stepped in before something irreparable could happen and brought you into your office, sat you down to relax until . . . I don't know . . . until something happened or changed."

Walker stood up and paced the floor. Embarrassed, he was trying to figure out how he would face his coworkers. "What else happened?"

"Well, you didn't know what a laptop was. I was going to try and explain it but figured it would be pointless or confusing, so I just redirected you from it."

Walker, feeling uneasy, sat back down and bowed his head toward the floor. "I . . . I don't know what to say. Sorry for putting you through this. Thanks for saving my ass."

Sheila got up, stepped behind Walker, and started rubbing his back. "It's okay. I'm just glad I got here before it got really bad."

"What am I going to do? I really need to get to the bottom of this before it permanently disrupts my life."

"I guess we'll have to see it to the end. I'll be here with you every step of the way. Soooo, what are you going to do about the day? Are you going out . . . there?" Sheila motioned her head as if Walker could see her do it.

"Nope. Right now, I'm too embarrassed to step out there. I think I'm going to hide out in here and wait until everyone leaves for the day."

"What about food?"

"Could you do me a favor and bring me some lunch? I would surely appreciate it."

"Sure, no problem. Well, I guess I need to get back to work myself. If anyone asks, I'll just tell them you're okay, and you'll explain what happened later."

"Thanks, I don't even know what to say or how to even explain it, for that matter. I'll just leave it alone and hope everyone will be reluctant to ask. I do need to apologize to Mr. Reese, though."

"I wouldn't," said Sheila as she walked toward the door. "Just leave it be unless he brings it up. Maybe he'll look at it as your being overworked."

"Yeah, you're right. Hey, I'll talk with you later?"

"Sure thing. I'll bring you some lunch in a couple of hours." Sheila opened the door and left. As she walked through the office, everyone was staring with the hopes of her giving them some kind of information. But she strode right past them without saying a word and opened one of the double glass doors to go to the other side of the building.

Inside his office, Walker went to his desk and pulled his laptop toward him, opened it, and began his work for the day.

***

The evening came quickly for Walker. He didn't notice the sun setting as he furtively worked. Walker decided, since he had what he now called "relapses," he would take the train home instead of driving. If for some reason it did happen, he didn't want to be behind the wheel of a car and endanger someone else's life.

Walker gathered his items and placed them in his briefcase, closed his door, and made his way down to the main floor of the building. He walked to the station so he could catch the 6:49 p.m. North Jersey Coast train to Edison, and he paid his fare. As he stood and waited, he noticed there were more people than usual waiting for the last train of the day. Fifteen minutes later, it finally arrived as his patience had begun to wear thin. Walker was one of the first to board the middle car and found two seats in the corner. The seat closer to the aisle looked wet, as if someone had recently spilled their coffee or some other beverage on it, while the other had a used newspaper sitting atop it. This was just fine with him, since he didn't feel like anyone sitting next to him and presenting the possibility of starting a conversation. All he wanted was to get home and get this day to an end.

Walker picked up the newspaper and sat down. As the train left the station, he began reading the discarded newspaper in the flickering lighting from the train car. The sun was nearly under the horizon as the train clattered to its next destination.

While Walker read the paper, it became noticeably dark outside. As he gazed out the window, he was disconcerted to see what looked like mountains. The sky was clear, and he could see snowcaps on top of the peaks from the full moon. As the train moved forward, it rolled into a tunnel, but not a modern city tunnel.

This one cut through the mountains. The sounds in the tunnel turned odd, changing from a quiet click-clack to a hard, rough clanking against the tracks, with a chugging choo-choo resonance enveloping his ears.

The clear sky became visible as the train pulled itself out of the tunnel. Light-gray wisps of smoke filled the colorless night sky. The car in which Walker was now sitting seemed to be from the early twentieth century. As he scanned the new surroundings, he observed that the attire on all the passengers had changed. Men were now in three-piece buttoned jackets with either bowler or top hats, while the women wore unflattering dresses with hats that looked as though they were from an old Easter parade. Even Walker's clothing was not how he was dressed when he'd boarded the train. They approached the railway station, and the platform was still made of concrete, but the construction was different. Since there were no longer side doors, the passengers were departing off the front and back of the car. Once the passengers who'd selected this stop departed, he heard the conductor bellow:

"Alle einsteigen."

Walker assumed it meant "all aboard," since he saw people rushing to get onto the train. He sat there in amazement as he took in the sights that now surrounded him. The train started with a slight jolt as it left the station. Walker looked out the window and saw vast patches of land with small cottages. The train traveled for what seemed to him like an hour before it made an approach to the final stop. He got up to exit the train. As Walker stepped off, his lungs inhaled the cleanest and freshest air they had ever experienced. He also felt more confident and very different from his normal self. It was as if he were still Walker but feeling the persona of someone else
at the same time. Hutchers seemed to be guiding him someplace, but Walker had no idea where. He entered the station and noticed men standing about with signage, and he noticed one in particular who had a sign with the name "Mr. Hutchers" written on it. Walker/Hutchers approached the man.

"I'm Hutchers."

"Welcome to Austria, Mr. Hutchers. I'm your driver, and I have a car waiting outside for you."

"Very well. Let's get on with it then."

"If you would follow me, sir." The driver gestured for Walker to walk with him. They went outside to a waiting car. The driver opened the door for Walker/Hutchers to get in. The driver closed the door and walked around to the front, got in, and started the car.

Walker was fully aware that Hutchers was in control and kept quiet to let Hutchers guide the journey. They made a thirty-minute trip on a winding, mountainous road, and a large mansion-like structure came into view.

Two men were standing on either side of a giant iron gate. Like clockwork, as the car approached, the two men moved to the front of the gate, grabbed a handle on either side, and pulled the double gates open. The car he was riding in went through the open gates without slowing down, and the gates were fully closed by the time the car was no more than fifty feet from the entrance. This efficiency amazed Walker, as he had never seen such precision before. The road, lined with birch trees on both sides, opened to a circular driveway and presented a huge mansion with two impeccably dressed men perched on either side of the doors, like statues. As the car came to a stop, another gentleman appeared from nowhere and opened the back door of the car.

"Good evening, Mr. Hutchers. We've been expecting your arrival." The man at the door bowed and gestured to beckon Walker/Hutchers out of the car.

He got out and made his way to the door. The crunch of the fine gravel in the driveway resonated in his ears as he walked to the front door. The dashingly dressed men opened and held the doors while he approached the inside of the house. The place was as immaculate as the men who surrounded him. A gentleman of stately features was waiting for him once he was inside the premises.

"Mr. Hutchers, welcome, and I'm so glad to meet your acquaintance," the man said as he bowed. "I hope your journey here was comfortable. We have a room ready for your stay. Please follow me, sir." The two men walked up the stairs into an elegant room. Another gentleman followed them and placed Hutchers's bag in the room.

"This gentleman, Mr. Shief, will make sure you have everything you need while you're here. If the room is not to your satisfaction, let him know, and we'll accommodate you according to your specifications."

Hutchers took a long scan of the room and was satisfied. "No, this will be fine. I have two questions. When is supper, and when will I meet the gentleman I chose as my butler?"

"There will be a reception at five p.m. whereas you will see your selected future butler performing his duties in training. His name is Albert Wrengould, and as you requested, he is not aware that he has been selected, but he comes from a line of servicemen in this field. The integrity of his family name is impeccable, and I vetted him myself. Supper is promptly at six p.m., which will be composed of a six-course meal. Afterward, we scheduled a meeting with you and the gentleman in question. If he is not to your liking, we have others in waiting."

"Very good," Hutchers said as he nodded in approval.

"If there's anything else you need, just pick up the phone," the stately gentleman said as he motioned to the phone with his gloved hand, "and Mr. Shief will be in to take care of it." The two gentlemen exited the room and left Hutchers to himself.

Hutchers was downstairs for the reception at 4:50 p.m. so he could see how the butlers in training carried out their duties when they were not under a watchful eye. He spied Wrengould walking and checking each table, along with checking each glass and all the dinnerware for perfection. He watched others but kept a close eye on the one who had been selected for him.

Hutchers decided to take it further and have small talk with him to see if he was suitable. After having a short conversation, he knew that Wrengould was exactly what he was looking for. The dinner following the reception was exquisite, and after the formal meeting with Wrengould, who was surprised that the man he had spoken with earlier was his possible new employer, Hutchers retired to bed so he could prepare for travels with his new employee the next day.

***

Walker woke up the next morning at home and in his bed. The last thing he remembered was the train ride.

"How on earth did I get here? This is embarrassing—and dangerous. I really need to get a handle on this."

He sat, trying to remember the events before he'd woken up. Now aware of his predicament, Walker was a little calmer but still apprehensive about where—and what—was happening in his life.

Okay, so coming home on the train and going through the tunnel is what I remember, Walker thought as he sat and looked out the window. When he closed his eyes, quick flashes of what seemed like movie clips flowed through his mind. Pixelated images slowly pieced themselves together of men in working tuxedos and a feast thrown together to help form a picture of what he'd lost during the last few hours. Muffled echoes warped into sentences and sounds that rang from his subconscious memories.

"Mr. Hutchers, I'd like you to meet Mr. Albert Wrengould. Because of the specifications you required, I feel he is the perfect match for you. Not

only has he been trained here, but his family, who has a long lineage of butlers, began training him when he was a child. His lineage has also served some of the most private and prominent families from around the world, so from these viewpoints, your privacy will be strictly adhered to with the highest confidence level."

"Yes, I talked to him briefly before the reception, and he impressed me during our conversation." Turning to the stately gentleman, Ferron continued, "You, sir, have picked a fine choice. There's no need for me to see any of the others. Mr. Wrengould, we will leave by noon tomorrow, so you should be prepared to do so."

Walker's subconsciousness started to ebb back to reality as it became apparent what he needed to remember. He retrieved his briefcase to get his laptop and the letter from the lawyer. He read the remaining clue of his puzzle and wrote the final answer on the document with the other answers.

Where did my butler come from and why did I select him?

I traveled to Austria to pick out my butler. His name was Albert Wrengould. I picked him because he came from a long line of butlers, and I did not want someone who worked for anyone before, with the confidence that they would keep my affairs private and without scandal.

Walker's head was hurting, so he decided to take this Saturday to relax and unplug from the world for the weekend. But before he relaxed, he decided to go online and book a flight from Newark back to Oklahoma for Tuesday morning.

FAMILY

Sheila was in her hometown of New London, Connecticut, on Saturday. She was sitting in her mother's dining room, waiting for her to come home from work. She looked around the modest house with the outdated furniture and started reminiscing about her childhood. She looked out the kitchen window and noticed the double swing set was still there. The chain on one of the seats was broken, while the other swung softly in the light breeze. As she watched the teetering of the swing, she became lost in thought until she heard the door lock unlatch. Her mother came in and was startled to see Sheila there.

"Wow! What a pleasant surprise! I didn't know you were coming to see me." Sheila's mom put her bag down and gave her a hug.

"Yeah," Sheila said as she embraced her. Her mother still wore the same perfume as she had when

Sheila was a kid, and it made Sheila feel a little bit at ease. Sheila pulled back from her mother and gave her a faint smile.

"So what brings you back here to this old place?" her mother asked as she sat down in the chair across from Sheila. The table sat four people, which was plenty for their family. The wood of the tabletop was worn from the years but still gleamed because her mom was obsessive when it came to cleaning.

Sheila sat back down and faced her mom. "Well, remember a while ago when I called and told you about my friend, Walker, and what he discovered?"

"Yes, I do."

Sheila took her mother's hands and held them. "I think the fight you and the family have been involved with for your granduncle's estate is about to become a little more complicated."

"What do you mean?"

"It's getting serious with Walker. He's been having more episodes and getting more clues about your granduncle Ferron."

Her mother's face turned to worry as she listened.

"How do you know that he's not researching and faking the whole scenario?"

"Because I was there a couple of times when it happened. I tell you, he was not himself! He talked differently, his attitude, even his walk! I had to quell an issue at work with him once because he got so . . ." Her voice trailed off as she started remembering the ruckus in the office.

"He got so what?" her mother asked, trying to get her back into focus.

"He was raging mad. It was uncanny. He scared everyone in the office, told his boss that he would fire him, as if he owned the place and that he took orders from no one. His attitude was like how I heard you talk about your granduncle."

Sheila's mother turned pale.

"This can't be true," her mother said as she shook her head in disbelief. "After all these years we've been fighting for this, some stranger might come and take it right from under us!" Sheila's mother looked at her. "I need you to tell me all about your friend so we can get the upper hand and be prepared in case we have to fight this in court."

Sheila turned from her mother and took her hands away. "Mom, I don't want to have anything to do with this. I just told you because I thought you should know. But as far as me passing along information, I don't want to do it. You're my family and he's my friend, and I really wouldn't feel right about getting in the middle of it all."

Sheila's mother looked dismayed, then angry. "Do you realize how long we've been fighting for this? Do you realize how much that estate could help this family? How can you? How can you pick a stranger against your family?"

"I'm not picking anyone over anybody, Mom. I just don't see what's the point of fighting for something that has not been successful for decades. Plus, I don't want any part of it! That money was not meant for us, and he made sure of it. I know you feel like it is because he was family, but from the reasons I heard when I was growing up, I can understand why he didn't."

"We had nothing to do with what happened to him." Sheila's mom was inflamed now. "That was our grandparents! Why should *we* suffer for what they did to him? That's our whole argument. Besides, who would be so selfish to will all his assets to himself and try to retrieve it when he comes back? That's the most absurd thing anyone has heard!"

As Sheila watched her mother go into a huge fit, she started regretting that she'd said anything to her. She thought she was being a good daughter and family member to tell her mother about the change of events. But she never expected this kind of reaction. Sheila was planning on spending the night, but now the tension with her mother was too high, and she would feel uptight for the whole time, so she decided to take the three-hour drive back home to Edison, New Jersey.

"Well, Mom, I just came to tell you what I know. I felt it was too important to talk about it on the phone, so I came here instead. I think I'm going to head back home. I have some things I need to take care of tomorrow." Sheila rose out of her seat and kissed her mother on the side of her cheek. "I'll be back to see you in a couple of weeks."

"Oh, I thought you were going to stay the night," her mother said, looking disappointed.

"No, but it was good seeing you, and I promise that I'll be back very soon. How's Jack, by the way? I haven't spoken to him in a while."

"Oh, your brother's fine. You'll miss him, though, because he was planning to come and see me next week. Maybe I can convince him to stay until you get back."

"That'll be wonderful!" Sheila exclaimed. "We need to catch up on each other's lives, anyway, so if you could do that, it'll be great!" After giving her mother a long hug, Sheila started walking toward the door, thanking herself that she'd absentmindedly forgotten to bring her bag out of the car. If her mother had thought she was spending the night, then leaving sooner than she'd planned would have made for an awkward moment.

***

As soon as Sheila started her car, her mother picked up the phone to call her brother.

"Phillip? It's Marge."

"Oh, hey, Marge. How're you doing?"

"I'm fine, but you're not going to believe what's happening!"

"What? What's going on?"

"Well, we may have a problem. My daughter's friend is claiming to be our late granduncle, and I think it's the real thing! We may be in trouble."

There was a long pause on the other end of the line.

"I think we better see the lawyer and try to reactivate our claim."

"But Phillip," Marge cried, "how could this be happening? There's no way someone can come back from the dead. What kind of man is he?"

Phillip sighed on the other end. "Look, Marge, the guy was off his rocker. There's no telling what he was into. No one knows, because he cut everyone off. Although I cannot believe it, this day was always a possibility. What, with the kooks that have tried for years, there was always a chance that someone would turn up. Whether he is Ferron or not, if the guy miraculously gets all the correct answers, then there's nothing we can do. Sure, we can go back to court and fight it, but . . ."

Marge stopped him before he could finish. "We waited far too long for some damn stranger to just pop up and take it from us. I want to fight!"

Phillip waited for her to finish. "The only thing we can do is just refile before he takes claim and see what happens, but, like I was about to say, I think it'll be a lost cause. I'll call the other family members and see what they say, then get back to you with the consensus."

They said their goodbyes and hung up. Marge stayed up for the rest of the evening, waiting for Phillip to call. She finally dropped into a deep sleep and was suddenly awakened by her phone at 11:00 p.m.

"Hello?"

"It's Phillip. I talked with the rest of the family, and they want to fight."

Marge almost jumped out of her skin at the news. This was what she wanted, and she was hoping the rest of the family would agree.

"Okay, when are we going to file?"

"We'll do it first thing Monday morning."

Marge was elated. "I'll meet everyone at the courthouse Monday morning. See you then." They hung up, and Marge looked at her weekend as being one of the best in a long time.

TRUTH

Walker arrived back in Bartlesville at the offices of Peason and Jeffers around 1:30 p.m. on Tuesday. He strolled to the receptionist and announced himself.

"Oh, Mr. Preston. Nice to see you again! I'll let Mr. Peason know you're here." She picked up the phone and made her call.

"Mr. Peason, Mr. Preston is here. Yes, sir. Yes, I'll send him in."

She put the phone down. "You can go in now, sir."

"Thank you," Walker said as he made his way to Peason's office.

Peason was sitting behind his desk when Walker entered.

"Hey, Mr. Preston. Great to see you again," Peason said as he came from behind his desk to shake his hand.

"Good to see you, too, sir," Walker responded as he reached to shake Peason's hand.

"How's everything going? I take it you've figured out some answers to the questions I gave you."

"Yes, I have." Walker was talking as he took a seat in one of the chairs in front of Peason's desk. "The process was . . . interesting, but I think I got the right answers you're looking for."

Peason had a peculiar look on his face. "Why do you say *interesting*?"

"Well, a lot of the answers came to me in . . . errr . . . dreams . . . or whatever they're called."

"How so?"

"The last one, for example: I was going home on the train and . . ." Walker's voice trailed off as he wondered whether he should try to explain it.

"And?"

Walker started to look uneasy but decided to go on. "And my whole vision turned into another area . . . another country . . . from long ago."

Peason sat up in his chair and indicated with a slight nod that it was okay to continue.

"I was in Austria from long ago, and I went to this place . . . huge estate where it seemed like a university of butlers. But as I appeared to be there, I was not. It was like I was being guided through the whole event. I woke up the next morning at home but have no recollection how I got there. Like I said, my last memory was at the estate."

Peason sat back in his chair and let out a slight sigh. "So you're telling me that you . . . you had some type of event that put you into a vision?"

"Not just a vision—it felt like I was actually there."

"So what did you get out of it? Did anything come to you that helped you in any way?"

Walker opened his briefcase. "Umm, yeah. It gave me the answer to one of your questions. It told me where the butler came from." Walker pulled out the piece of paper he'd printed with all the questions and answers on it. He handed it to Peason. "I think I got everything right, but I'm not sure."

Peason took the document from Walker, and as he read each question along with the answer, he lost all the color from his face.

"This can't be true!" Peason jumped out of his chair and quickly went to the bureau to open the safe, which held the original questions and answers. He scanned the twenty questions for the four he had given to Walker. As he read the answers next to each one, he almost fell over and could feel his mouth getting dry. "Mr. Preston . . . I . . . I've never seen anything like this. Sir, it appears that you answered each question. You not only answered them, but you did so word for word!"

Walker was astonished and said something totally out of his character. "Does Don Canton still work here?"

Peason turned quickly to face Walker. "Wait . . . how did you . . . how do you know that name?"

Walker offered a knowing smile. "Because he's the one who witnessed the signing of my documents."

"Your documents?"

"Yes. Canton, your father, and my doctor were all in here when it came time to set everything up."

Peason hurriedly sat back down at his desk. "Mr. Hutchers?"

"Who did you think it was, lad?" Walker's voice and demeanor changed. "How's your father, boy?"

Peason flushed with surprise. "That actually was my great-grandfather, and he passed a very long time ago, sir."

Walker/Hutchers regarded Peason with a faraway look. "I gave him the money to start this firm, you know. That's why I let him and no one else handle my affairs."

Peason's color drained from his face. He was whiter than a ghost shining in the dark.

"What's the matter? Did you think I would not come back? I'm sure no one did, but my belief was too strong not to," Hutchers said as he got up to walk around. "I remember when he bought this desk, and I had this bureau made per my instructions. That was crafted specifically for my documents."

"Sir," Peason started, seeming unsure of whom he was talking to, "the family is trying to fight your will and trust. As a matter of fact, they filed just yesterday to contest all that is happening right now."

Walker's/Hutchers's face turned to disdain. "How dare they! Don't they remember who I am? They'll get not one penny from me or my estate! That family abandoned me, and when I tried to help them, they took advantage. No, they will not succeed. They will not win, and they will be miserable for the rest of their lives!"

Peason appeared taken aback. "Sir, I've already taken the liberty of countering everything and asked for the first scheduled court date available. We will get this squared away at the most expedient time we can."

"I see your descendants taught you well. I hate waiting for anything, and you're doing exactly as I would have expected. I do have to ask you, though: How have my companies been doing? Have any of them faltered?"

"Oh, no, sir. They have flourished! Every company has done well. I believe you'll be very satisfied with the growth of all properties and assets you left in our care. My descendants followed all your instructions about what kind of executives you wanted for each asset in your portfolio, and they not only met but exceeded our and your expectations."

"Very good! What is the total value of my assets?"

"Well, sir, from last quarter's accounting, it's at forty billion."

Walker's/Hutchers's eyes twinkled. "I would like to see the balance sheets, please."

Peason responded carefully. "Sir, per your instructions, we are not to show you anything concerning the assets until everything has run its course through the courts."

"Very good. They *did* teach you well." Walker/Hutchers smiled. "Well, I see you have everything handled here. I'll be on my way and await your call about when we're due in court." Walker/Hutchers got up from the chair and started toward the door. He turned around. "Mr. Peason, I appreciate everything you're doing for me to settle this. I couldn't imagine in my wildest dreams that something like this could happen to me."

Peason was again taken aback, because now it was Walker talking to him. "Mr. Preston?"

"Yes, Mr. Peason?"

Peason looked at Walker with a serious expression. "I believe you.

DISMISSED

Thursday began normal for Walker. He was back home in Edison, New Jersey, and relieved that he was finally able to figure out what had been happening to him for most of his life. Although he was still in shock, he felt at peace with the outcome of the events that had come about. *I need to thank Sheila for putting me on this track; otherwise I don't know what would've happened for the rest of my life. I also cannot believe that somewhere down the line, court willing, I'm about to become a billionaire. Who in their wildest dreams would have thought something like this? And I didn't even believe in this reincarnation stuff!*

Walker was almost at work after parking his car in the garage across the street when he saw a black sedan slowly following him. Although he spied it from the corner of his eye, he knew that it was matching pace with his steps. He got his confirmation when he stopped in front of his building and the car stopped too. He saw two men in the front seat and a woman in the back. Walker tried not to pay attention to it, but he had a feeling it had something to do with everything that had been happening to him. As he touched the handle of the building's door, one of the men and the woman got out of the car and called his name.

"Mr. Preston. Mr. Preston! Wait, can we speak with you for a moment?" The woman was holding her purse as they dodged people walking on the sidewalk.

Walker turned around when he heard them calling him. As they approached, Walker released the handle and stayed on the outside of the building. "Yes, what is it?"

The woman seemed to be in charge. "Hi, I'm Marge Crowder, and this is my brother, Phillip. We have an issue that I would like to see if we can discuss."

155

Walker eyed them suspiciously. "What kind of issue?"

"We're descendants of Ferron Hutchers, and we hear that you are in the process of taking claim of his assets."

"Wait, how did you find me?"

"Oh, I'm Sheila's mother. Hutchers was my maiden name. She told me about your ordeals and quest for finding clues to the questions that have been at his lawyer's office for decades. I don't know how you did it, but I think you're a fraud, and I'm going to prove it."

Phillip looked on as his sister was talking. Although of above-average height and weight, he was a meek man, so he let his sister do all the talking. He just stood by her side and nodded while she continued berating Walker.

"This is a family issue, and any stranger that thinks they're going to come and impede on something we've been fighting for years for and take it all away has another think coming!"

Walker was starting to feel agitated. One, because these people stopped him on what had started to be a great day. Two, this was not the time or place to discuss something like this, especially since he was getting ready to present his project to the execs of the company. He had no time to deal with this, but someone else did.

Walker's face contorted, and his body became rigid, as if his posture was changing. His voice became acidic, and his words were so caustic, if they were liquid, the strongest barrel would not be able to hold them. "Now you look here, Marge . . . Phillip, not the lot of you would *ever* get your gritty little hands on my money! Since my family did nothing to make sure I was safe and secure, what makes you think I would ever consider making your life or any of your descendants' lives happy and carefree off my success? You think you're miserable now, keep fucking with me and see how much more pain you and your bunch would endure. Now get the hell off my property before I have you arrested and your car towed and crushed!"

Marge and Phillip were aghast. Both stepped back and subconsciously grabbed each other to run to the car.

Walker smirked as he watched the disheveled pair hurry to their car. Walker opened the door to enter the building. Hutchers walked through the lobby. As he glanced around the perimeter inside the building, Walker tried to take back control, or at least attempted to control the actions of Hutchers. He forced his alter ego to stay quiet while he moved through the lobby and to his office.

Walker entered his office successfully. Hutchers stayed at bay, and no one said a word to him as he walked past. He sat behind his desk to prepare for his presentation with the executives. Walker gathered his files and walked to the conference room. Everyone was already there, so he opened the door and made his way to the empty chair with a placard bearing his name.

"Good morning, everyone," Walker announced as he made his way to his seat. Some nodded almost in unison while others replied back. He opened his files and picked up the remote in front of him for the projector. "Our client wanted specifics to find what assets they needed to move to expand their operations.

As you know, they have an expansive portfolio. It took a lot of time and hard work with the team we selected to tackle this task, but I feel we got it on the money, so to speak." A slight chuckle fanned the room from one of the oldest accounting jokes around. "As the blue highlight lines indicate, these properties and assets have been on a decline for the last three years, and their expenditures have been increasing. So it's safe to say they can be reallocated into a new portfolio that will be ready for dismantling and-slash-or sale."

Everybody nodded as Walker continued his presentation. An old rival of his, David, who always had questions that either did not make sense or were delivered just to get under his skin, cleared his throat. "Ahem, excuse me, Walker, but I see you have a couple of assets here that don't make sense. You say that this one lined as 3C is not profitable, but four years ago, it had a better return than any of the active assets. Why did you put that on there when it's possible that it could regain strength in the market?"

Agitated, Walker turned in his direction. "Because our goal was to find assets that have not been doing well for three years, not four. It was in agreement with everyone on the team. Now if anyone has any other questions . . ."

David interrupted again. "But why did you decide on three years and not four?" Walker could feel Hutchers trying to come out, but he fought him with everything he had. "Again, that's what the team decided, not me."

"But if it was only one year . . ."

"Look here, you lazy son of a bitch," bellowed out of Walker's mouth before he could catch it. "You couldn't count your way out of a coffee satchel with one bean in it! How are you going to comment on something that's out of your depth?" Walker walked over to him and put his face right into David's. "You're so much of a loser that your wife is screwing *him*!" Walker pointed to an exec who went beet red. There was no control now. Hutchers came into full form in front of everyone. "As a matter of fact, you *all* are a bunch of losers. I should fire every . . . single . . . last . . . one of you."

Nobody moved. At first, everyone was shaking, but a couple of the higher execs regained their composure and remembered what their positions were.

"Walker! How dare you speak to us like this!" one of them finally screamed. "This is way above insubordination. You will apologize at once to everyone in this room!"

Walker/Hutchers stared at the man with the most irate and coldest look. "I speak how I want. I do not apologize, and I most certainly am not a subordinate to anyone! You, sir, if you are that, have *no* authority over me. I have all the authority and will see you out of this building at once!"

The exec quickly stood up out of his chair. "Mr. Preston, you are really crossing the line."

"Mr. Preston?" Walker/Hutchers said with a sneer. "My name is Ferron Hutchers!"

The exec's eyes widened. He'd heard that name before but could not believe it. "What kind of tricks are you pulling here, Walker? Someone call security and get this man out of here. Now!"

One of the aides in the room picked up the phone on the conference table and spoke quietly. Moments later, three men in uniform appeared at the double glass doors and opened them. The exec pointed at

Walker. "Remove this man from the building!" Two of the guards approached Walker and wrestled him into a hold to take him away. The third held the door open to let them pass through.

"What do you think you're doing?" Walker/Hutchers squawked as the two men carried him to the door. "Take your filthy hands off me! How dare you even have the gall to touch me!"

After the two guards made their way through the glass doors, the third rushed past them to retrieve the elevator. Walker was screaming insults and obscenities to no one and everyone. Once they reached the lobby, another guard was waiting downstairs with Walker's briefcase and a box of his belongings.

"You can't throw me out of my own building! This will be the end of all of you!" Hutchers was driving Walker's body, and Walker could not control him. But the recollection of Herbert flashed in his mind, of how he had been removed from the company.

I guess this is the price of karma for Herbert. Walker saw things through Herbert's eyes and realized how terrified he must have been. Although Hutchers was in complete command of their predicament,

Walker felt remorse about how Herbert was treated. Once the guards reached the door, they put Walker down and ushered him out, personal items and all. They closed the doors behind him and stood on the opposite side until they saw him walk away. As soon as the air hit Walker, Hutchers left his presence. Walker stood on the sidewalk, dumbfounded. He realized he was without a job. Walker bowed his head and a sullen mood enveloped him as he made his way to the garage.

AFTEREFFECTS

Walker sat in his apartment in the dark for the entire weekend. He could not believe that he no longer had a job. He was dismal. Although many tried to reach him, Walker would not answer his phone. But he knew he had to rejoin the world sometime, so on Monday he got up to make lunch. As if on cue from his thoughts, his phone rang. "Hello?"

"Mr. Walker, this is Mr. Peason."

Walker perked up a little, hearing his voice. "Oh, hi, Mr. Peason. How are you?"

"I'm doing well, sir. Listen, I was calling to tell you that I have an expedited hearing for you so we can try to get this matter closed quickly."

Walker breathed a sigh of relief. Not only was he out of a job, but this whole ordeal was beginning to ruin his life. "When is it supposed to happen?"

"Can you get here by Wednesday afternoon? I have it set for Thursday morning, but we need to do some preparation before we go."

"Sure, I mean, I'm not doing anything else. I haven't caught you up with the latest events in my life. I got fired from my job a few days ago."

Peason sat silently on the phone, then said, "Wow, I'm sorry to hear that. What happened?"

"Mr. Hutchers happened. I was in the middle of doing a presentation, and this one guy who really gets under my skin was questioning my team's work process. I tried to ignore him, but ole Ferron Hutchers came out of nowhere and ... well ... he basically verbally pummeled the whole executive team. I got escorted out."

Peason absentmindedly let out a slight whistle. "Sir, after this I don't think you'll have to worry about another job for the rest of your life."

"Oh, there's one other thing. His relatives came to see me on that same day. That's what triggered the whole episode."

"You're kidding me, right? How did they find you?"

"You remember my friend Sheila? Apparently, Ferron Hutchers was her great-granduncle. Her mother is his grandniece. She told me she was part of his family after we came back from seeing you."

"Now this is a surprise! Do you think Sheila told her what's going on?"

"It's her mother," Walker exclaimed. "So I'm sure she did."

"What are you going to do about her?"

"Nothing, when she told me about it, she was pretty embarrassed. She knew about the money through her family and never wanted to have anything to do with it."

"Okay, have you spoken to her since you had the confrontation with them?"

"No," Walker said as he held the phone a little tighter, "but I'm planning on calling her today to meet up with her. I have not spoken to anyone in a few days."

"Are you planning on bringing her with you? She'll be a good witness to attest to a lot that you've been going through."

Walker pondered before he answered. "I don't know. I'll see what happens after we talk."

"Well, let me know, because I will have to prepare her also if you decide to use her." Peason paused and spoke again. "I'll talk with you later, Mr. Preston. I hope you have better days until then."

"Thanks. You have a good day too." Walker hung up the phone and dialed Sheila's number.

Sheila was sitting on her couch and picked up the phone when she heard it ring. "Hello?"

Walker was a little hesitant before he spoke. "Hi, it's Walker."

Sheila spoke excitedly, then with concern. "Walker! Hey, are you okay? I tried calling you several times after I heard what happened at the office, but when you didn't respond, I figured I'd let you get in touch with me when you were ready."

"Yeah," Walker slowly answered, "that day was a rough one. It . . . it was one of the worst days of my life. Can you come over so we can talk?"

"Sure," Sheila said. "I'll be over in a bit."

"Thanks, I'll see you soon." Walker hung up and continued to the kitchen to make lunch, as he'd planned before the phone call from Peason.

A while later, Sheila knocked on Walker's door. He walked over to answer it. "Hey, Sheila," he said as he gave her a hug. "I made us lunch."

"Oh, good. I'm starving. I was just about to have something before you called, but since we haven't spoken in a while, I thought that I would rush on over."

Sheila came into the apartment.

"Soooo, how have you been?" she asked as she made her way to the kitchen.

Walker followed her as he responded, "I've had better moments in my life."

Sheila sat down on the stool opposite the kitchen cutout separating the dining room from the kitchen, as Walker grabbed the two plates of sandwiches, chips, and bowls of fruit he'd prepared earlier.

"Thanks for this." She picked up one of the sandwiches and began to eat. "I heard what happened at work. I'm so sorry you were fired for it. Was it like before . . . when I came to assist you?"

Walker stayed in the kitchen on the opposite end of the counter. "No, it was worse, so much worse. But before I get into that, I need to tell you that your mother and your uncle came and paid me a visit at work that morning."

"Oh no!" Sheila gasped. "What in the world!"

"Yeah. Hey, did you tell her about what has been going on with me and this whole ordeal?"

Sheila put her head down, guilt ridden. "Yeah, I did. But it was only because I thought they needed to know. I didn't realize she would come here and confront you about it. But what happened?"

"Well, she did. I was having such a nice morning, and all of a sudden I see these two people walk up to me and harangue me like never before."

"Oh my! They're so obsessed with this that it makes me sick!" Sheila's face turned into one of disgust.

Walker continued, "The thing is, I just wanted to go inside and not be bothered, but Hutchers came out and took care of it. He basically scared the hell out of them."

Sheila perked up as she heard this. "How so?"

Walker had that faraway look in his eyes. "He told them in so many words that no matter what, they won't get ahold of anything regardless of how hard they tried, and he warned them not to pursue it."

Sheila sat there, shaking her head. "I just don't understand them. They've been at it for years. What makes them think that something's going to change?"

"You're right, little girl. Nothing's going to change!" But Walker's voice had.

She looked at him with a glint of shock. "Walker, are you okay?"

"Not Walker. Hutchers. And who are you? You look mildly familiar."

Sheila seemed to realize what was happening and switched with him. "Mr. Hutchers, I'm Sheila. Remember? I helped you in your office a while back."

"Oh, yes, yes. Now I remember. You helped me look for my files and ledgers. I like how you stepped up to the plate while everyone stood there, cowering. But what are you doing here?"

Sheila decided to try something. "Mr. Hutchers, I'm a friend of Walker's ... and your great-grandniece."

"Wait! Are you one of my no-good relatives that's trying to steal my money?" Hutchers started becoming agitated upon the realization of who she was and her connection to him.

"Oh no ... no, Mr. Hutchers. I never wanted anything to do with any of that. I heard the stories growing up, and I thought the way you were treated as a kid was terrible. It disgusted me, and I thought my family was wrong for trying to win the suit for your possessions for all these years."

Hutchers still eyed her suspiciously. "But like I said, what are you doing here?"

Sheila hesitated. "Well ... as I said before, I'm Walker's friend. He asked me to come over. I was concerned about him after what happened during his presentation, and this is the first time I was able to speak to him."

Hutchers grinned slightly. "Yeah, that was a spectacle. But having the gall to throw me out of my own place! They will pay for that ... dearly!"

Sheila sat, transfixed by his transformation and was ready to accommodate both personalities.

"So, you say you're my great-grandniece ... and Walker's friend? What are the odds of that? Let me ask you a question, little miss."

Sheila was intrigued by what was happening in front of her, but she had to stay focused in case things turned the other way. "Yes, Mr. Hutchers. What is it?"

"Did you help me in the office because I was Walker or because I was me, Hutchers?"

Without hesitation Sheila exclaimed, "I helped because he's my friend. I didn't want him getting in trouble because I knew he needed his job. But I also helped because I knew what was going on with him, and I couldn't just sit there and do nothing."

As they talked, Hutchers became more relaxed with Sheila. She told him about the advancements that were made in the world, including the contraption he'd seen . . . the laptop . . . and how powerful it was for finding information and using it for business and entertainment. She told him about current events and politics.

Hutchers listened intently and was pleased, amused, and at times shocked, especially about the advances of technology. Hutchers began to tell her about his life, but Sheila tactfully got off the subject. "Mr. Hutchers, I don't want to sound rude, but there's a lot going on, and if I knew anything about you, it could jeopardize what's about to happen. Plus, although I do not agree with what my family is doing, I'm close to my mother, and I'm afraid if you tell me something, it may slip out while I'm having a conversation with her, and they would be able to use it."

Hutchers was pleased and understood her reasoning. "I can see you're not like the rest of your relatives and that you care a lot about Walker. I'm not a trusting soul, never really have been, and if you know my story like you say you do, you can understand why. But I'm starting to like you, and if Walker trusts you, then I should too."

Sheila gasped. "So you're aware of what's going on? That you are here . . . with Walker?"

"Oh yes, I've been aware since I saw your mother and uncle. Something between us triggered me to come out. Although Walker was not aware that this had happened until he . . . well, we were being escorted out of the building." Hutchers/Walker got up from the stool opposite Sheila and came around to her side. "He'll need you as a witness to get all this settled, so don't disappoint him."

Sheila appeared flabbergasted with this new awareness and by how alert Hutchers was inside of Walker. "Mr. Hutchers?"

"Yes?"

"How long are you planning on being around? I mean, now that you're aware, are you planning on sticking around?"

"Oh no, dear child. Once everything is settled, I'll be gone. Walker is aware of my presence, but I can come and go as I need to. I want this proceeding to happen without a hitch. After that, Walker can do as he pleases."

Sheila breathed out a sigh of relief.

"You're right. It's not going to change. That's one of the reasons I wanted to talk with you and thought it would be better for me to ask you in person." Walker was back and continued the
conversation as though nothing had happened. Sheila changed with him to match the present person and conversation.

"Sure, what do you need?"

"Mr. Peason called earlier. He told me there is a hearing on Thursday but would like for me to get there on Wednesday. He also thought you would make a great witness, and both he and I would like to know if you would be able to come, so he can prepare us. If so, we would have to be there by Wednesday afternoon, which means, of course, we'll have to be at the airport early that morning again."

Walker was now standing in front of Sheila. She took his hands in hers. "Sure, whatever you need. You know I'm here for you."

Walker felt a warmth coming between them as reassurance emerged. "Thanks, I really appreciate it. You don't know how much this really means to me."

Sheila felt his genuine sincerity. "You know I got you."

READINESS

Walker and Sheila were sitting in Peason's office at nine thirty Wednesday morning. Peason was sitting across from them, files strewn across his desk. Peason began, "Thank you two for coming. We have a lot of ground to cover before tomorrow, so let's get started."

Peason opened one of the folders in front of him. "This is the suit that the family filed last Monday to contest our findings for our case. As you can see, their main argument is that you researched and fabricated your answers to receive something that does not belong to you. They are also claiming you acted under false pretense to become Ferron Hutchers in front of others to validate your claim. Now, we all know this is not true, and I have no doubt that we will win."

Walker and Sheila listened intently as he explained the proceedings and how they would take place.

Peason showed them the documents he'd prepared, which included the original documentation left by his great-grandfather and Mr. Hutchers, the questions and answers Walker had given him, and the original version of the recording Walker had received from the psychologist.

Peason turned to Sheila. "I need to prepare you for tomorrow. Even though everything falls on Walker, you're an integral part of this process. Not only because you witnessed what happened and can attest to it, but because, well, it is your family that we are going against. So before we begin, I need to know what your feelings are on the whole matter."

"Well, Mr. Peason, Walker is my friend, and I've seen him go through this ordeal since I've known him. I'm glad that he finally has answers and will support him as much as I can. Although that's my family and I love them dearly, it seems like I'm going against them, but what's right is right. If Mr. Hutchers made the decision not to give them anything, then that's how it is."

"I'm glad you feel that way, but I have to tell you, you'll have the toughest time on the stand, because your family *will* look at it as a complete betrayal."

"I understand, and I'm ready for the consequences."

"Good." Peason nodded. "Let us begin." Mr. Peason pounded question after question at Sheila. Her confidence in answering each one amazed both Peason and Walker. He started with light questions, such as how long she had known Walker and the details of their relationship. Then he hit her with hard and confusing inquiries. But she was stable and handled all of them like a pro. After Peason was satisfied, he stopped. "Sheila, I think you're prepared more than you think, and I feel you will do great on the stand."

"Yeah," Walker said. "I'm impressed! You know more than I thought you did."

Sheila said with a slight smile, "Well, a lot of it was too memorable to forget."

Walker nodded and felt a slight flush.

Peason watched the interaction between the two and didn't want to interrupt but felt it necessary. "I think we've done enough here for the day. We have to be in court at nine a.m., so I need you two to get some rest, because I'm sure it's going to be a very trying day." Peason got up from behind his desk and walked around to bid them farewell. Walker and Sheila followed suit and sat up as well.

Peason extended his hand to shake theirs. "Okay, Walker . . . Sheila, it was good seeing you again, and I'll see you tomorrow. If you can get there by eight thirty a.m. so we can get the last-minute kinks out of our system, that'll be great."

Both exchanged handshakes with Peason, and Walker spoke when he took his hand. "That'll be fine. We'll see you at eight thirty."

"Super, I'll see you then. Take care, you two."

"You do the same," both said in unison. They left and walked to the hotel. Once there, they prepared to unwind. Sheila said what Walker was thinking. "I'm hungry. I think we should get something to eat."

"Yeah, me too, but I don't really feel like going back out. I think we should order room service."

Sheila thought for a moment. "Yeah, I think that'll be a good idea. My brain hurts from all those questions, and if it's going to be like that tomorrow, I'd rather rest and be refreshed so I can tackle whatever comes my way."

"Good idea," Walker said as he picked up the menu. He studied it and made his choice, then handed it to Sheila. Once she decided what she wanted, he picked up the phone and called in the order. After he put the phone down, Walker turned to Sheila. "If I haven't told you before, I want to say thanks for always being there for me. This has been an ordeal, and you definitely saved my ass a couple of times. I honestly don't know what I would've done if you hadn't been around."

Sheila placed her hand on his shoulder. "I'm glad that I'm able to be there. You are not only my best friend, but you were once my lover, and even though we're not together, I still feel a lot for you."

Walker put his hand around her waist and gently pulled her toward him. "And I still feel a lot for you too. Even though it didn't work out back then, I appreciate that we stayed friends and in each other's lives."

Sheila was about to respond, but Walker pulled her even closer and began to kiss her before she was able to utter a word. He picked her up and moved toward the door of the suite's bedroom. They never heard room service knock on the door.

THE TRIAL

Walker and Sheila arrived at the courthouse at 8:30 a.m. sharp. Mr. Peason was already in the hall, waiting for them. "Walker . . . Sheila! Good morning. Glad to see you. Are you ready to start the day?"

They both looked at each other, then turned to him and nodded. "Yes, we are." Walker said, "I want to get this over with. But I can't believe I'm actually here doing this. All this from a recurring dream. Who would've thought?"

"Believe me," Peason answered, "it's been a long time for this firm too. I didn't know if I would see this happen in my lifetime, but I was on the verge of preparing my daughter to be the next one to take over, if warranted. But now I don't think that will be necessary, because I'm perfectly convinced that you are Mr. Hutchers. If I could get on the stand myself, I would."

Walker beamed at the confidence. "Thanks for saying that. It means a lot to me."

"Hey, no problem. I saw what happened with my own eyes, and I'm a very practical man. So if I'm convinced, I can't see how no one else would be. But now, it is up to the courts. With that said, we should go ahead and make our way to the courtroom."

The three of them walked toward the wooden double doors. As they approached, they saw Hutchers's estranged family walking from the opposite direction. When Sheila's mother and uncle saw Walker, they had the most worried, frightened looks. Then they saw Sheila, and her mother's expression changed from frightened to one of the iciest stares she could muster. Sheila attempted to speak to her mother, but her mother just continued to walk and ignore her as Sheila stood next to Walker and Peason.

Walker took her hand. "Don't let that bother you. Just be strong and do what you think is right. If you feel like you need to not go through with this because of pressure from your family, I'll totally understand."

"No," Sheila said as she squeezed his hand, "I'm where I'm supposed to be. I'll be fine." The three of them walked into the courtroom. As they moved down the aisle, they could feel the eyes from their opponents as if they were stabbing their very souls. They sat down on their side of the courtroom and waited for the judge to arrive.

Low murmuring and slight conversations could be heard throughout the courtroom as the judge entered and sat at his bench. The bailiff's thunderous voice silenced everyone. "All rise!" Nothing could be heard but the rustling of clothing and objects shifting, along with the movement of the chairs against the blue industrial carpeting as everyone stood up. "The District Court of Washington County in the state of Oklahoma is now in session, Honorable Judge Newross presiding. You may be seated," the bailiff pronounced. The judge looked at the documents pertaining to the trial as he began to speak. "Good morning, ladies and gentlemen, this is case number 20-63119402: Marge Crowder et al. versus the Estate of Ferron M. Hutchers and Walker Preston."

The judge continued to look through the documents. "I see this case is about the validity of the defendant being . . ." He paused as he looked further at the documents and saw it was a case he'd never seen before. "The reincarnation of Ferron M. Hutchers?"

Peason stood and spoke, "Yes, Your Honor," and sat back down.

"And the plaintiff is contesting the validity because of the circumstances surrounding the proof?"

Mr. Blake, the family's lawyer, stood and spoke. "Yes, Your Honor."

The judge took a few more moments to look at the documents again. "Well, this is a most unusual case. Even though it is, we will only look at the facts and decide by those only. Are the plaintiffs ready?"

Blake, Marge, and Phillip stood as Blake answered, "Yes, Your Honor." Then they sat back down.

The judge turned toward Peason's area. "Are the defendants ready?"

Everyone at Peason's table stood, and he answered the judge. "Yes, Your Honor." They returned to their seats.

The judge nodded. "Let us begin and hear the opening statements."

Blake stood and approached the podium. "Your Honor, ladies and gentlemen of the court, we are here to disprove the nonvalid claim of the estate of Mr. Ferron Hutchers by the defendant, Mr. Walker Preston. Mr. Preston claims he is the reincarnated self of Mr. Hutchers. Mr. Preston also claims that he has answered questions to clues that have not been broken for decades. We are here to prove this is not the case and that he possibly received answers to some of the questions from his witness, Sheila Crowder. We are also here to prove that he knew nothing about Mr. Hutchers and that he researched all the information to falsely gain access and claim to the assets of Mr. Hutchers. I mean, who in their right mind believes that someone can . . . come back from the dead? We will prove this is not the case and the claim as a whole is a fraud."

The lawyer stood at the podium for effect, then slowly walked back to the plaintiffs' table.

Peason watched the family attorney as he made his way back to the plaintiffs' table. After Blake settled,

Peason got up and began his opening statement. "Your Honor, ladies and gentlemen of the court, I want to point out something my fellow colleague over there said. Mr. Preston claims that he's the reincarnation of Mr. Hutchers." As Peason talked, he looked at each and every person in the room, including Sheila's family. He was careful enough to begin with a pause before staring at the family and performing his visual sweep. "Mr. Walker Preston *is* the reincarnated Mr. Hutchers. I say this because I know for a fact that the evidence will prove this is the case. But even if it wasn't, there were processes put in place for whoever made the claim to show proof . . . without a doubt and without error to verify that they are Mr. Hutchers. Mr. Preston has proven to me and my firm beyond a shadow of doubt that he is the right claimant. Forget about the reincarnation factor, although that can be proved. The fact is that Mr. Preston passed all the requirements necessary to be the rightful person to the claim. Since the time the will had been sealed, no one has ever answered all the questions set forth, let alone come even close. Mr. Preston answered everything without a hitch. Now they claim he has no rights to this fortune. But let me ask you this. If *they* had any right to it, or were able to prove any of the answers to any of the questions set forth, wouldn't they have it by now? The case, although it can be proved, is *not* if Mr. Preston *is* Mr. Hutchers, but did he follow and pass all the legal obligations set forth to be awarded the claim. The answer to that question is absolutely! So let us go forth and let the facts decide, and everyone can move on with their lives."

Peason walked back to the defendants' table. As he did so, he took another look at the opposing family and gave them a slight wink. The cold emotion from that side of the room was enough to make the sun freeze.

"Mr. Blake, call your first witness," the judge announced. Mr. Blake called Marge to the stand. Marge walked over and swore the oath. Afterward, she sat on the witness stand.

Blake began. "Good morning. Please state your name for the court."

"Marge Crowder," she replied.

"What is your maiden name?"

"Hutchers," Marge responded.

"And what would you like to tell me about your family?"

Marge sat uneasily in the chair. "Well, we had a family member named Ferron Hutchers who passed years ago. He was very wealthy, but"—she paused—"when he died, we found out he left all his assets to himself. Didn't leave the family a thing. The way he left his will and trust was . . . it was . . . rather strange and unorthodox, even for him."

With a solemn face Blake looked at the audience in the courtroom, then to Marge.

"How was it strange and unorthodox?"

"Well, our dear relative, whom we all respected, left everything to *himself*!"

Blake favored her with a puzzled look, more for effect for the court. "Wait, you say he left everything to himself? How in the world was he able to accomplish that?"

"He designed a will and trust with instructions that when he came back to this world, all his assets were to be restored to him."

"Restored to him? What kind of method did he use to achieve such a thing?"

"He . . . Ferron . . . believed in reincarnation, and he put in his instructions that when he was reincarnated, he would get everything back. I mean, who has heard of such a thing?"

Blake turned to look at the judge, then back to Marge. "Surely your family thought this was impossible and tried to fight these instructions."

"Yes," Marge answered. "But his lawyers wouldn't budge or compromise. I mean, we loved Ferron, and we know he loved us, so we were shocked and dismayed that he did his family in such a way."

Blake ended his questioning with Marge. "Thank you, Mrs. Crowder, that's all I have for you." Blake made his way to the plaintiffs' table.

"Cross-examine, Mr. Peason?" The judge looked over his way, and Peason started getting up from the defendants' table.

"Yes, Your Honor, I would." Peason walked over to the witness stand. "Mrs. Crowder. May I call you Marge?"

"Umm, yes, you may."

"Okay, Marge," Peason began. "How many times would you say your family contested the will?"

Marge looked up at the ceiling as she tried to remember. "I'll saaaaay . . . about five times that I can recollect."

Peason turned to the people in the courtroom. "It was twenty-five times that we counted since Mr. Hutchers passed. And during these efforts, the court has turned you and your family down every time. Now you said your family loved Mr. Hutchers and he loved your family?"

"Yes, yes, we did, and yes, he did."

"Then why did he not leave anything for you or for anyone else in the family, for that matter?"

Marge hesitated before answering, but before she could, Peason pounced. "I'll tell you why. Because you were not as close as you say. As a matter of fact, he had no contact with your family for almost the entirety of his life!"

Blake jumped up. "Objection, Your Honor. He's badgering the witness!"

The judge was about to say something, but Peason

responded first. "Your Honor, I'm merely trying to point out the witness's fallacy in her statement. Mr. Hutchers was very much estranged from his family and therefore would have never given consent to any of his assets because of past occurrences with said family."

The judge overruled Blake's objection. "I'll allow it because it does show relevance as to the nature of the relationship."

On cue, Peason turned and stated, "I have nothing further for this witness."

"Does the plaintiff have any redirect questions?" the judge asked.

Blake declined. "No, Your Honor."

The judge turned to Marge. "You may step down, ma'am."

Marge pulled herself out of the witness stand with her head down. As each family member took the stand, Blake asked them similar questions, and to a few he asked more detailed ones. But when it was Peason's turn to cross-examine, the grilling of each witness was like a charbroiled steak on an open fire.

Once everyone was done on the plaintiff's side, the judge called a recess for lunch.

Peason, Walker, and Sheila went to the nearest café to eat. Walker and Sheila sat across from Peason in a booth and discussed the day so far.

Walker spoke after they ordered their lunch. "Wow, that was pretty intense."

"Yeah," said Sheila. "I kinda feel bad for them. They really have no case or reason to think they'll win."

"Don't get too confident," Peason noted. "We still have to do our part, and depending on the judge, things still could go their way. Our strategy should work if we stick to the plan. Now remember, they also have a right to cross-examine, and you two have to keep your calm when it does happen."

Sheila and Walker both nodded. They wanted this to be over with, but not in a way where it could jeopardize the case. So they agreed to be patient and confident when it was their turn to get on the stand. About forty-five minutes later, they all hiked back to the courthouse for the second part of the day. Sheila's family was already there, sitting in their place. As before, the family looked in their opponents' direction as if they wished they would have driven off a cliff during the break. Walker sensed Sheila's nervousness and took her hand under the table to calm her down. It seemed to work, because he could feel her slight shaking subside. The bailiff came out and did his usual procedures, and the judge called the court to order.

"Mr. Peason," the judge announced, "call your first witness."

Peason rose and walked to the podium. "I call my first witness, Sheila Crowder."

Sheila rose out of her chair and walked to the witness stand. After she was sworn in, Peason began his questioning.

Peason moved to the direction of the witness stand and stopped when he was a friendly distance from Sheila. "For the court, could you state your full name?"

"Sheila Louise Crowder."

"Ms. Crowder, could you tell the court the name of my client and the relation between the two of you?" Peason was always careful not to call Walker "the defendant."

Sheila looked toward Walker and smiled. "That's Walker Preston, and he's my best friend."

"How long have you known Mr. Preston?"

"About two years."

"And could you tell the court your relation to the plaintiffs."

Sheila looked at her family. "Yes," she said slowly, "that's my family."

A low murmuring spread across the room after Sheila spoke. Sheila nervously looked around the courtroom as the commotion continued, but Peason stared at her until her eyes met his, and he gave her a warm and reassuring smile, with a nod that signaled she was doing well. This calmed her again.

"Why are we here in this courtroom today, Ms. Crowder?" Peason asked with a soft tone.

Showing more confidence, Sheila answered, "We're here to prove that Walker is the heir of Hutchers's estate."

"Ms. Crowder. May I call you Sheila?"

"Yes, sir."

"Sheila, could you explain to the court how you, a

friend of Walker's, can actually prove that he is the heir of Mr. Hutchers's estate?"

"Well," Sheila began slowly, "I was around when he answered a couple of the questions that needed to be answered."

"What questions are you referring to?"

Sheila looked at Walker, then to her family. "When Mr. Hutchers was alive, he set up a will and trust. When he did so, he also placed a series of questions with instructions for someone to prove it is him coming back to life . . ."

"Reincarnated?" Peason interrupted.

"Yes, reincarnated. He left a set of instructions and questions for a person to prove they are him . . . Mr. Hutchers."

"And did Mr. Preston show this proof?"

"Oh yes! Not only did he prove it, but he answered them all correctly."

"Sheila, how did he find out about Mr. Hutchers? Did you ever mention him to Mr. Preston?"

"Umm, no."

"But you've known him for two years. Surely you had to mention him to Walker sometime during that time."

"No," Sheila responded. "I never talked about my family to him, or to anyone, for that matter," she said as she lowered her head. "All that was too personal and convoluted for me to bring up to anybody."

Peason walked closer to the witness stand and placed his hand on the banister. "So how did Mr. Walker come to know about Mr. Hutchers?"

"Well," she said with slight hesitation, "ever since I've known him, he kept having this . . . nightmare."

"Nightmare? Explain to the court what you mean about this nightmare."

Sheila looked at her family and then to Walker. "He continued to have a nightmare about someone dying in a fire. It would wake him up in the middle of the night, and through the years, it got worse."

"And how do *you* know about these nightmares?"

She continued to look in Walker's direction. "Because I was with him when some of them happened."

Peason turned toward Walker with a sullen face, then back to Sheila. "Did you do anything to help him with his nightmares?"

"Yes, I gave him a card to see a psychologist."

"And did he go see that psychologist?"

"Yes, yes, he did."

"What happened when he went to see this psychologist?"

"He got hypnotized and found out at that time that he was Ferron Hutchers."

Blake jumped out of his chair. "Objection, Your Honor! Objection! That is purely hearsay!"

"Mr. Peason."

Peason turned to the judge. "Your Honor, I'm trying to establish how we came to the point of why we are here. As a matter of fact, I have a recording of that session here with me. If it pleases the court, I would like to play it."

"Overruled, Mr. Blake. Mr. Peason, if you have evidence of the recorded session, you may play it."

Blake sat down, clearly steamed.

Preston went to his briefcase to produce the flash drive with the recording on it. As it played, gasps went through the room. Family members who were young enough to know what had happened sat up straight in their seats. The room was silent after the recording played, and everyone stared at Sheila, then Peason, and finally Walker. Although most were behind him, Walker could feel every pair of eyes on him, and it made him uneasy. After a slight pause, Peason turned to Sheila. "Is this the same recording you heard in my office that Walker Preston gave to me?"

"Yes, it is."

"In your recollection, does any of it remind you of any part of his dream or nightmare that he described?"

"Yes."

"Did you help him with any of the questions I gave him to answer?"

"No, Mr. Peason. I did not."

"I have no further questions for this witness. Thank you, Sheila." Peason walked back to his side of the room and sat next to Walker.

The judge turned to the plaintiffs' table. "The plaintiff may cross-examine the witness."

Blake had the look of a shark smelling the copper hint of blood in the water. He rose from his table and walked quickly toward Sheila as an intimidation tactic.

"Ms. Crowder, you said you've known Mr. Walker for two years?"

"Yes, sir."

"And how did you meet him?"

"We work in the same accounting firm."

"Work in the same accounting firm," Blake said, repeating her statement and pausing for theatrics. Then he walked closer to the stand and got into her face.

"Did you, Ms. Crowder, set up a plan to retrieve these assets with Mr. Walker by feeding him information about Mr. Hutchers that you may have found out about but didn't tell your family so you could keep the estate for yourself?"

Peason jumped up. "Your Honor, objection! He's reaching!"

Before the judge could respond, Sheila raised her hand to stop all the commotion.

"No, I did not. We became friends, dated, and broke up, but we're still friends."

"Are you still friends because you continue to have a plan to receive the fortune for yourself and shut your family out of the process?" Blake asked accusingly.

Just as cool as she could be, Sheila responded, "I never wanted anything to do with any of it. Our meeting was happenstance. But I will tell you this. From what I saw, he is Ferron Hutchers. I've seen with my own eyes what has happened to him." Then she looked at her mother and pointed. "She knows it." Then to her uncle. "He knows it, too, because they both saw it for themselves when they confronted Walker at his job. Did they tell you that?"

Blake turned around and looked at the pair, seeing them staring icily at Sheila. The looks were so cold he felt a chill from them. He turned to finish with Sheila and ignored her statement. "Did you or did you not tell your mother what was happening with Mr. Preston?"

"Yes."

"Did you do it out of guilt or to gloat that you were about to have the family fortune at your feet?"

Sheila started to answer, "Well—"

But before she could, Blake interrupted. "No further questions. I'm done with this witness." Blake walked back to the plaintiffs' table and sat next to his clients.

"Does the defense have any redirect questions?" the judge asked Peason.

"Yes, Your Honor. I have."

Peason stood up. "Ms. Crowder, why did you tell your mother about the events surrounding Mr. Preston?"

"Because although I didn't agree with my family's decision of what they were doing, I still felt it was my duty as her daughter . . . as a family member . . . to let them know what was going on."

"Thank you, Ms. Crowder. No further questions." Peason sat back down.

The judge looked at Sheila. "You may step down, ma'am." Sheila rose and walked back to the area reserved for her side. "You may call your second witness."

Peason stood up and walked back to the podium. "I call Mr. Walker Preston to the stand."

Walker rose and moved forward to the witness stand. Once he said his oath and sat, Peason began. "Can you state your name for the court?"

"Walker Preston."

"Mr. Preston, I'll get right into it. How did you learn about Ferron Hutchers?"

Walker gave a long sigh. "Well, since I was a boy, I kept having this nightmare of a man dying in a fire on some stairs. It subsided as I got older, but for some reason, about two years ago, they started coming back." Walker looked in Sheila's direction with a hint of surprise, because he had just realized something. "As a matter of fact, it started happening again after we met!"

Sheila gasped, and everyone in the courtroom started murmuring. The judge banged the gavel to quiet the room. "Orrrderrr!"

Walker started again. "As time went on, the dream became stronger, and it caused a rift in my relationship with Sheila . . . Ms. Crowder over there." He pointed in Sheila's direction. "One day I was at work, and I had some type of episode, which was embarrassing."

"What happened at work, Mr. Preston?"

Walker looked down and continued, "I passed out, and it was from something that I couldn't explain, but I knew it had to do with the dreams."

Peason appeared concerned. "And what did you do afterward?"

"I had a talk about it with Sheila, and she recommended I talk to the psychologist that she mentioned to me earlier in the day. So, reluctantly, I went to see him. At that point I was hypnotized and found out I was Ferron Hutchers in another life."

Peason took the flash drive. "Is this the recording of your session that I played earlier?"

"Yes, it is."

"Objection, Your Honor. I haven't been able to prove the validity of that recording," Blake shrieked.

"Sustained—you'll get your chance to argue it during cross," the judge replied. Blake sat back down and sulked as he continued to listen.

Peason picked up from where he left off. "What did you do afterward?"

"I didn't know anything about Mr. Hutchers, but I researched him and found all this . . . stuff out about him. During my research, I saw that your law firm was handling his affairs, so I visited your office to talk to you about it."

"And then what happened?"

"I . . . I told you what transpired, but you didn't believe me. I told you that he traded something to someone else. You were surprised that I knew this information . . . and I was surprised that it was the answer to one of the questions. Questions that I knew nothing about. After that, you gave me a set of questions that I needed to answer to prove that I was Ferron Hutchers. I got back to you with those questions answered, and here we sit."

"Did Sheila ever provide or entice you with any information about Mr. Hutchers?"

Walker looked at Sheila, then to her family and back to Peason. "No. As a matter of fact, I had no idea she was even related to him . . . Mr. Hutchers . . . until she told me after our first meeting at your office."

"So, Mr. Preston, how *did* you come up with the answers to the questions I provided to you?"

Walker started feeling uneasy because he knew this was going to be a stretch. "Welllll," Walker rubbed the back of his neck and could feel the hint of droplets on the nape of his neck. "They came to me in a series of . . . I guess dreams and episodes."

Peason stepped closer to the stand and put his hand on Walker's shoulder. "Can you explain, son?"

"They just happened. Came on their own. I had no control over when or where they would happen. I would get images, sometimes scenes or whole stories."

Blake sat straight up. "Your Honor, objection! This is ridiculous! No one is to believe he got his answers from some . . . visions? What's next?"

Before Blake could ramble on, Peason's voice overpowered his. "Your Honor, these are Mr. Preston's recollections. Who is Mr. Blake to say what is and is not in this man's mind or what he experienced?"

"Overruled. Unless you have proof of him not experiencing his account of events, then we will move on. Continue, Mr. Walker."

Blake sat down wide eyed, as if he could not believe what was happening.

"So," Walker continued, "a lot of these episodes gave me the answers to the questions you gave me."

"And I want to reiterate, Sheila had nothing to do with giving you any of those answers."

"No, sir, she had nothing to do with it. As a matter of fact, except for the question I answered in your office, she does not even know what the other questions were or the answers I came up with. You're the only one I shared them with."

"Your Honor, I have the flash drive that we heard earlier and a signed affidavit from the psychologist who recorded the session. Along with this, I also have notarized documents. I'd like to place all this as evidence for the court. They are the will and trust for Mr. Ferron M. Hutchers, which includes the affidavit of his mental and physical health at the time the documents were drawn up, the instructions he set forth, the series of twenty questions and answers that Hutchers developed, and the four required questions and answers that Mr. Preston answered flawlessly." Peason handed all the documents and the flash drive to the bailiff, who handed everything over to the judge. "With that, I'm done questioning my witness." Peason sat back at the defendants' table with Sheila.

The judge continued with the next process. "Mr. Blake, your witness to cross-examine."

Blake sneered as he looked at Walker, appearing as though he wanted to shred and erase Walker's story as much as he would like to shred the documents and erase the recording that had just been entered into evidence. "Mr. Walker, you claim that you were having dreams about Mr. Hutchers. Is that right?"

"Yes, sir, I was."

As he came closer to Walker, his voice became stern. "And you claim that during these . . . uh . . . hmm . . . dreams, you received answers to questions that *nobody* in decades has been able to answer."

"That's correct, Mr. Blake."

Blake's voice became harsher. "How do you expect anyone to believe that you, Mr. Preston, came up with all this information that nobody else has been able to? You're in collusion with the young Ms. Crowder over there"—he pointed in Sheila's direction—"to take hold of a fortune that neither of you have rights to! Those answers, fabricated! That recording, fabricated! For all we know, that recording is staged! You, sir, have nothing to do with anything that's involved in this case except for a bunch of fabricated information that you created for your benefit. This case should be settled in my clients' favor, and you should be brought up on charges for fraud!"

Walker sat there, listening, having his character admonished by a perfect stranger. He tried to stay calm and wait for this barrage of insults to end. But Blake kept on until Peason stepped in. "Your Honor! Mr. Blake is off the rails here!"

Blake turned to Peason: "You are probably in on it and should be disbarred!"

Peason, normally calm, lost his cool. "How dare you! You are the most unprofessional lawyer—"

"How dare *all* of you!" The unfamiliar voice came out of nowhere, but it reverberated from where Walker was sitting. Everyone turned in his direction as he stood up and leaned over the witness stand with his palms on the railing. He turned to Blake with a seething look and fire in his eyes.

"You have no clue of what the fuck you're talking about!" this new person said as he met Blake's eyes.

"I'm here to tell you what's going to happen!"

The judge raised his gavel but appeared to think better of it and decided to wait to see how it would play out.

"I'm Ferron Hutchers, and you people have no clue what's going on here. I created those documents! I gave Walker those answers because . . . I . . . am . . . here . . . inside of him. We are one. Marge, Phillip, I knew you greedy sorts would try to grab hold of my fortune. Your grandmother came to me long ago and swindled money from me when I had a moment of weakness and tried to help! So you can thank her for you not getting a dime!"

Marge and Phillip were visibly shaking.

Blake began to open his mouth. Hutchers saw it and whipped his whole body toward him. "You sorry piece of shit. You must've gotten your law degree as a prize out of a Cracker Jack box, because your theories are nuts!" He then turned to the rest of the Hutchers/Crowder family. "And you! Not one of the lot of your families wanted me when I was at my lowest. I mean, for the love of life, my father was gone. My brother and mother had died, and your families left me out in the cold. I had to fend for myself and was barely a teen. So for that, I did everything I could to make sure you would never be able to prosper. Have any of you noticed how hard your lives have been? That's because I did it. I put processes and events in place to make sure you would never succeed. Because I owned a bank, I made sure to get any loan you applied for. Your properties are on a long-forgotten process of perpetual loans that you would never be able to get out of unless you could come up with full payment of the property, which you will never be able to do!"

Everyone, including Peason, could not believe what was happening. Hutchers looked over to Sheila, and he softened. "You are always kind to Walker. You were kind to me."

Someone on the family side exploded. "This is a farce! I knew this was a setup between you two. I'm sorry, Your Honor, but can't you see they're playing us?"

Hutchers/Walker grew beet red. "Farce? Let me tell you about farce, Andrew!"

Andrew sat there, now still as a stone.

"Your great-grandfather ran away with my mother's sister after he came to me for money. Did your grandfather see him again after he told him he was coming to see me? No! But why did I make the rest of you suffer, you may ask? Because I wanted your family to feel the same pain I did when *your* great-grandfather never came back home to his family. . . just like my father. They were brothers, and both had the same trait. Leaving their family to rot as they led their new lives."

Andrew tried to stifle a tear, but one came down, presumably prompted by stories of his great-grandfather leaving and the difficulties his family had faced.

Hutchers had a slight grin as he watched the change in Andrew. "How does it feel, Andrew? Bringing back old memories, eh? Good! Anyone else want to say anything?"

No one else dared to utter a word for fear of Hutchers telling their secrets in court to others who knew nothing about them. Once he knew he had the floor again, he continued where he left off and turned back to Sheila.

"As I was saying, Sheila, I was in a spot and did not recognize what was going on. But because of your kindness to your friend and then to me, you have my gratitude. You are nothing like the rest of your family. You have such a kind heart. You taught me things about what is going on in the modern world, and no matter what, you were never intimidated by me. Your patience gained my trust, and as I said, you have my gratitude."

Hutchers then looked at Peason. "I want to thank you for keeping my instructions to the letter as I directed to your great-grandfather, right along with looking to continue the tradition that I set forth. Because of that, your firm will always have the business of my assets and trust. The documents are already drawn up and hidden in a secret compartment in the bureau of your office, which I had designed for your great-grandfather. It was placed there before it was delivered, and even he did not know about it. Open the left door, tap on the top-left corner, and the inside panel will open with those documents in it."

Appearing overcome, Peason nodded and thanked Hutchers for continuing to trust his family. Hutchers turned to the judge.

"Your Honor, I want to attest that I am indeed Ferron Hutchers. As you can see from my estranged family, they now agree and no longer have any fight left in them." Hutchers turned to them, and they all put their heads down, because they knew they were defeated. "My story is a complicated one, and the details are both exciting and sad, but the man who is here is the one to take claim of my assets."

The judge, still in disbelief, tried to regain his composure. He looked at the documents Peason had given him as evidence and noted one thing. "Mr. Hutchers, just for my sense of validity, what was your brother's name?"

Hutchers looked at the judge as he answered with a tear in his eye. "Robert. His name was Robert."

REWARDS

"Mr. Blake, sir, I'm not in any collusion with Sheila. We had no idea that . . ." Walker continued with his answer to Blake as everyone watched. Blake stood in front of him, trembling. Walker stopped talking and looked around the courtroom. Everyone was looking at him in total astonishment. He did not know what they had just witnessed, so he had no idea what was happening. Walker looked at Peason, then to the judge. The judge had a sincere but solemn expression.

"Son, there's no need for any more testimony. I'm ruling in your favor."

Walker was still dumbfounded. He was wondering what had happened in the last two seconds of Blake asking him a question. Little did he know that ten minutes had passed. He looked over at the family and saw nothing but fear and shame. "I ... I don't understand."

The judge continued to look at Walker. "Mr. Preston, are you aware of what happened in the last few minutes?"

"Yes, Blake was accusing me of collusion, and I was about to answer him."

"No," said the judge, "we met Mr. Hutchers. If I were not here to witness it myself, I would not have believed it. But the fact is, your proof has been established, so there is no need to go any further with this case. You will be awarded everything that was once his. You may step down from the stand."

After Walker sat down with Peason and Sheila, the judge continued, "In the matter of case number 20-63119402, Marge Crowder et al. versus the Estate of Ferron M. Hutchers and Walker Preston, I rule in favor of the defendants. This case is now closed!"

With the sound of the gavel, it was over.

Just like that, Walker was a billionaire. Peason got up and feverishly shook his hand, and Sheila gave him the biggest hug ever. "We did it! We did it!" Peason said as Walker stood there, still in disbelief.

"I'm so excited for you, Walker!" Sheila exclaimed as she continued to hug him.

"We have some unfinished business to take care of at the office, Mr. Preston. I have paperwork for you to sign so we can release all your funds, holdings, and assets to you. We'll go over everything so you can be aware of what you have, and it's massive."

Walker heard him but could not move. The air around him exploded with an outbreak of excited conversations around the room. People were talking about the events of the last final moments. Some came to congratulate him, while others looked at him like he was from another world. Reporters who were there and thought it was going to be a mundane court proceeding wanted to interview him. No one noticed Peason on the phone, but a few moments later, four men in dark suits waded through the crowd and came toward Walker. "Sir," said one of them, "we were hired to be your security for the duration of your stay here."

This was too much for Walker, and his head was swimming. *I can't believe this!* he thought. *This is going to take some time to get used to.* Walker turned to speak to Peason. "Is all this necessary?"

"Yes. You are a very rich man now. You have no idea how much so."

As if on cue, the men gently surrounded the three to usher them out. "Sirs, ma'am, if you can come with us, please. We have a vehicle waiting outside." They were soon ushered out of the courtroom with everyone following them. Everyone except the dejected family was leaving. They just sat and watched the people leave as despair enveloped the whole family like a dark phantom. For fear of embarrassment, no one dare moved until the last footsteps left the room.

Outside, Walker, Sheila, and Peason were placed in a huge SUV and whisked away as the crowd huddled behind and on the sides of the vehicle, peering inside and trying to get a final look at the new billionaire.

Walker was exhausted. As the car drove to the law office, he was feeling more spent than ever. But he knew he had to get everything done before something else happened. The SUV pulled in front of the law office and everyone got out to enter.

Once inside, Peason went to the bureau Hutchers had gotten built for his great-grandfather and pulled out the second letter Hutchers had written to whoever was awarded the estate. He then followed the instructions told to him by Hutchers. When the panel opened, an envelope dropped out. No one, not even his descendants, had known this was in there.

The document laid out instructions for his firm's continuing business relationship with whoever made claim for the estate. Peason placed the document on his desk so he could review it more carefully later. Peason stepped over to Walker and handed him the envelope that was for the claimant. "This is the second letter that Hutchers wrote to whoever won the claim."

They both sat down in their usual spots in front of his desk. While Peason went to his computer to print the necessary documents for Walker to sign, Walker opened the envelope.

To the new recipient of my assets, I know it has been a journey to reach this point, but I want to let you know there is no one or nothing that will be able to take what you just

*received. I am not sure if I may have invaded
your life, but if I did, it was for affirmation
that you are indeed me reincarnated. I
amassed all this for myself, and because I
was so strong in the belief of returning and
the way I had to grow up, I was never
planning on sharing it with anyone but
myself. Now I do not know who I will be in my
next life or what my demeanor will be. I will
not let the demeanor of my present be a ruling
factor of yours. Once you have control of
everything, you can do as you please with no
interference from me.*

Ferron M. Hutchers

Walker put the letter back in the envelope and
placed it in his inside pocket, deep in thought. Sheila
reached over and grabbed Walker's hand. "So how
does it feel? To finally have all this over with?"

Walker looked at her with a hint of surprise. "It
feels surreal. I mean, I don't understand. I was about
to answer Blake, and the next thing I know the judge
is ruling in my favor."

Peason looked up and interrupted. "Yeah, well, you lost some time while you were on the stand. Hutchers came." Peason began to tell him all that he'd missed. He told Walker what Hutchers had revealed about the family and what he'd done to keep the family from having successful lives. He also told Walker how Hutchers had announced to the judge who he was and how the judge had asked Hutchers his brother's name. Afterward, Hutchers left.

Walker sat there glued to every word, not wanting to miss any detail. "Wow, so he was still manipulating things even though he was no longer around? This is . . . I don't know what to say. I kinda feel bad for the family now that I've heard all this. I just hope it's all really over and he doesn't return now that the proof has been established."

Walker felt Sheila squeeze his hand a bit more. She sat for a few moments before revealing her piece of information. "Walker?

"Yeah?"

"Remember the last time we were in your apartment? When you called me to come over?"

"Yes, I do."

Sheila took a deep breath before she began. "Well, you turned into Hutchers in the middle of our conversation. I don't think you were aware of it, because you continued where we left off after you came back."

Walker looked dazed. He slid his hand from Sheila's and put his head in his hands. "Man, I'll be so glad when all this is over."

"That's what I wanted to tell you. He asked me to come to court with you because, somehow, I gained his trust. He wanted me to be your witness. He also said once everything was finalized, he would not be returning, and you can do as you wish."

This set Walker at ease, as it revealed the same thing as in the letter. Then he realized that this part of his journey had ended. "Hey, Mr. Peason, can we get something to eat?"

"Yeah, I am a bit hungry," Sheila agreed.

"Sure," Peason replied. "I'll have my assistant order something while we work."

Peason took their requests and called his assistant to put in the order. As they worked, Peason began going over the documents, explaining each one in

221

detail to Walker. Walker's head started spinning as Peason pulled out spreadsheet after spreadsheet.

Luckily, he was an accountant, so it was easy for him to decipher. Still, he could not believe how much he'd amassed just from a single court case. He noticed an asset that he was familiar with and some that put him in distress. *This is entirely too much,* he thought as he pored over document after document.

They continued to work as they ate their dinner. After everything was finalized, Walker received a secured flash drive from Peason, with everything he'd just seen. "So that's everything?" Walker asked.

"Yes, sir, it is," Peason replied as he gathered the original signed papers and placed them in a folder to put back in the bureau made specifically for Hutchers . . . now Walker.

"Great!" he said. Walker looked at Sheila. "Could you excuse us for a few moments?"

Unsure of what was happening, Sheila nodded. "Sure." She got up and headed to the door.

Walker looked at Peason, worried. "I need you to do something for me."

"Anything, Walker."

"I need you to draw up some more paperwork and deliver them accordingly."

Walker gave Peason his instructions, and as Peason jotted them down, a concerned look crossed his face. "Are you sure you want to do this?"

Walker looked at him seriously. "Yes, I am."

"Okay, I'll have this drawn up and delivered as quickly as possible."

Walker got up to shake his hand. "We're going to catch our flight in the morning so we can get back."

Peason chuckled. "Catch your flight? Sir, you have a private jet! I took the liberty of ordering you a new one once you gave me your answers."

A private jet? No more standing in line at the airport? "Thank you! Thank you for everything! I was skeptical about this whole thing, as I know you were, but you gave me the benefit of the doubt, and I appreciate you for it!"

"It was my pleasure. I can't think of a better person to receive it. After everything you have been through, you definitely deserve it!"

"Thank you again. And let me know when that paperwork is sent out."

"I most certainly will."

Walker took one more look in the office. This was where his life changed. His eyes became watery as he made his exit to the door. Sheila was waiting on the other side, lying on the couch in the reception area. She had dozed off while Walker and Peason were in the office. Walker went to her and gave her a slight shake on her shoulder.

"Sheila, wake up," he whispered.

She slowly opened her eyes and saw him.

"Is everything okay?" she said sleepily.

"Everything's great! Guess what?"

Sheila pulled herself up from her reclining position on the couch. "What?"

With a grin bigger than his face could hold, he said, "I have a private jet!"

"What?"

"Yeah!" Walker said excitedly. "I told Peason we were going to catch a flight tomorrow, and that's when he told me!"

"Wow!" Sheila said excitedly. "That's . . . so . . . awesome!"

He pulled her up from the couch and looked lovingly in her eyes. "Look, Sheila, I don't think I could have done any of this without you. As I look back, this was the root of our relationship going sour, but despite all that, you stuck around and were still my friend. I appreciate that. Now that all this is over, I would love to try again with you."

"Oh, that would be wonderful! I never stopped loving you," she screamed excitedly.

"Good, I'm happy you have the same feelings as I do. But we need to get back to the hotel and get some rest, because I have something I need to do at home." With that they left from the law office on their way to the hotel.

***

The following Tuesday morning, there was a lot of commotion at Walker's old office. Someone had called an executive meeting, but no one there could figure out who. They all sat in the conference room, talking and speculating. Some thought there were going to be layoffs; others thought someone else had bought the company. Whatever it was, everyone in the boardroom was nervous. The glass double doors opened. Walker and Sheila entered with two security guards. No one recognized the guards, but they knew the other two. Some of the execs were about to boil over when they saw him.

"Walker! What the hell are you doing here?" one of them asked accusingly. You have no right to be here!" The exec stood up and pounded both fists on the table. Walker looked at him with the most unassuming look.

"Sir! Sit down!" one of the guards said. Although the exec didn't know who they were, it scared him because the man's voice vibrated around the room. Walker walked to the head of the table and sat down. Sheila took the empty chair next to him. Everyone gasped because they were wondering what he was doing.

Wasn't he fired? one person thought. *And he has the nerve to sit at the head of the table?*

Some fidgeted nervously as Walker opened a folder that he'd carried in with him and began. "First, let me apologize for what happened the last time I was here. But, in a sense, that was not me. Although the story is unbelievable, I inherited this company."

He gave the folder to Sheila, and she handed each one a copy of a document.

As they read it, people shuffled in their seats. His manager looked on, wide eyed. The exec who'd had him removed had sweat pouring down his face. Walker waited until the reality of the situation sank into everyone in the room. David, his interrupting nemesis, felt a dire sense of panic, knowing this would be his last day.

The exec who'd kicked him out spoke first. "But how . . . ?"

It would be too difficult for him to explain, so he came up with another answer. "The person who originally owned this company was Ferron Hutchers. Unbeknownst to me, we were . . . related. I just found out last week."

The exec turned pale white as he listened.

"I'm here to let you know that nothing will change." He looked at David. "All positions will stay in place, but some attitudes will have to be adjusted." His stare let David know whom he was directing that to. Then he looked at Sheila. "Sheila here will no longer be working under you. She'll be working with me now instead." He felt no one needed to know about their relationship until he was ready to reveal it. "Now I'm going on a long, well-deserved vacation. Any inquiries you have, you may contact her."

Sheila's phone was buzzing. She looked at her screen and saw it was her mother. Sheila excused herself and mouthed to Walker who it was. He nodded and smiled as she walked through the doors.

Sheila was unsure as to the phone call. She had been convinced she wouldn't hear from her mother for a long time after what had happened. "Hello?"

"Sheila! Oh my God! Sheila!" her mother shrieked over the phone. "You won't believe what happened!"

Sheila was startled by how her mother was talking. She thought the worst and waited for her mother to tell her someone had died.

"Mom? What . . . what happened?"

"Your friend! Oh my God, it's incredible. Some of us in the family received a package this morning by courier. When I opened mine, it was the deed to the house . . . paid in full. With a check for a nice sum of money! I got a call from your uncle, and he received the same thing. We called the other relatives who had property, and every last one of them got the same package!"

Sheila could not believe her ears. That must be what he had been doing in Peason's office while she had been outside.

Her mother continued, "He sent everyone the same note and it reads:

"To the Hutchers extended family. I am sorry for the pain you endured for all these years. Although this cannot take the hurt, anger, and despair away, I wanted to give each and every one of you this gift to make your lives easier. Those who do not own property, your checks will be arriving soon, but I wanted to immediately take the burden away for those who did."

She turned and looked back into the room at Walker, tears streaming down her face.

Walker looked at Sheila and smiled. He turned back to the execs in the boardroom. "Sometime in the future your questions will be answered, but again, I want to assure you that nothing will change." With that, he rose and walked out the door.

Upcoming novel

by

Emmanuel Campbell

THE MUTED

THREE FIFTY-SIX P.M.

The arid land near Antelope Mountain in Utah, held a secret that a lot of people were not aware of. It contained a Deep Underground Military Base or D.U.M.B. which consists of a civilian/military science center. It was buzzing with people in both civilian and military attire. Their focus was the sun, and the recent activity they had been monitoring for the past few months. It had signs of elevated sunspots and a Coronal Mass Ejection, known as a CME for short, that could possibly reach earth. The average person or astronomers would not know about these particular sunspots because the staff in the facility have been very careful not to divulge exactly what coordinates they were locked on. Besides, with the state-of-the-art DARPA equipment that was being used, no one else would be able to notice what their test results were proving time and again. The CME that was expected to hit today at 4:13 p.m., had a factor that alarmed everyone in the room. The President and his Chief of Staff, along with the top military brass, knew about it and its possible consequences, but it was decided not to tell the world about it. There was one person who tried to warn people by way of a secret podcast he started, but he mysteriously disappeared, because no one in the facility knew they were being monitored to squash incidents such as this. After he was eliminated, they took his voice print and created scripts that were used on the podcast to make him sound like a rambling, unstable person, so those who started to believe what he was saying would think he was just another person with nothing to do but spread falsehoods.

The CME, on this particular day and time, from this particular region of the sun, will not only have an effect on the electronics that the world has never experienced, but this CME will also have a devastating significance on the human body. Although, they are not sure what it will be. This particular team found something in the plasma of this expected CME that would alter the DNA of anyone who may or may not be in contact with an electronic device. They just were not sure what *kind* of effect it would have.

General Tom Albertson, who was in charge of the facility, didn't agree with what his superiors were doing, and their decision to keep it a secret. But he was a staunch military man, and in his career, he learned to follow orders as directed, no matter how much he opposed of those decisions. But this particular directive did not sit well with him. General Albertson looked solemnly at his peers in the room as he wondered what the world would look like and how much of an impact this event will have in the next fifteen minutes. He saw the worried looks on everyone's faces because he knew they were worried about their families. He pondered on it, then made a decision that may ruin his career. The buzz in the room was noisy, so he spoke as loudly as he could.

"Can I have everyone's attention please." he bellowed out. The noise in the room settled down to a hush. The only thing you could hear was the gentle rush of air coming thru the vents which kept the atmosphere at a good seventy degrees in this underground and sealed chamber.

"First, I want to thank everyone for being here despite what we know. Now, I know all of you have families that you're worried about and we have been sworn to the highest level of secrecy. I too, have family out there, so I understand what you're going through. So, I decided for the next ten minutes, I'm going to let you reach out to your families so you can tell them not to use any electronics for the next half hour. However, you are not authorized to tell them what we know. We know that something is going to happen when this CME hits, but still not sure what, and because of this, I, like yourselves, want to protect those who we love. The last five minutes before the event, I will need everyone back to doing their jobs because those will be the critical moments."

Everybody looked around and couldn't believe what they were hearing. They immediately stopped what they were doing and started calling their families. All you heard were hush conversations and the repeated digital sounds of phones being hung up. By 4:08 p.m., everyone including General Albertson, made as many phone calls as possible and most were satisfied that they were able to reach all who were the most important to them. Before the event, mostly everyone was back in their positions within the five minutes as directed by Albertson. One station was still empty. Huddled in a corner, David Eggloft was still talking on his phone. He had a large family and wanted to reach as many as possible. Although time was critical, he tried to wait until the last minute so he could reach as many people as he could. He continued to talk to his brother so as to convince him to do as directed.

"No John, you don't understand what I'm trying to tell you. I don't have much time, but I need you to stay off the phone after we hang up for a while. That meeting can wait until after that time."

"But this call is the opportunity I have always been waiting for! Something I've been waiting for all my life! I can't reschedu…" suddenly as the lights darkened in the room, David's line went dead. He looked at his phone and noticed that it didn't have that usual glowing hue you would normally see in the dark. The room was pitch black and not a sound was heard.

The air stopped circulating, but there was enough of it in the room to accommodate all for 3 hours. Just like everyplace else in the world, all electronics in the facility failed when the CME hit the earth. Within forty-five seconds, the air ducts expanded a familiar whirl indicating the controllers were about to send in new fresh air, the lights slowly dimmed on one by one while the monitors and computers began rebooting. General Albertson let out a big sigh of relief. Once they knew what was going to happen, Albertson scrambled for the last three months to harden the backup electrical and electronic systems that would be able to withstand the strongest EMP and CME pulses. Everything came back online as planned.

Meanwhile, David got his bearings straight. As he looked at his cellphone, he saw it staring blankly back at him. He stuffed his phone into his pocket and got up from the corner where he was hiding to go back to his station. He punched in his password to get his monitor to display his data and continue his tasks. His job was to monitor power surges and drops as the CME moved across the earth, but now he was behind because he was trying to convince his brother to stay away from electronics. General Albertson walked over to his station to see what kind of readings he received. "Eggloft, what's your SITREP."

Eggloft began to speak, but nothing would formulate. Not...one... sound...came out of his mouth.

"Eggloft, did you hear me? I need your SITREP."